Noelle Forrest—Denver's "Dinosaur Lady." She's a paleontologist, but she's been more successful *talking* about dinosaurs on TV than actually digging for them. But young Jason Reilly may change all that when he brings her a fossil he found on Matt Caldwell's ranch. He may change her life in other ways, too—by introducing her to Matt, for one thing. *And* by appealing to maternal instincts she's hardly aware she has!

Jason Reilly—Life hasn't exactly been kind to this eleven-year-old boy. He's in foster care because his parents abandoned him. A few years ago he had an accident that left him using crutches and a leg brace. But Jason's a survivor. And he's very sure of two things: he wants to be a paleontologist like the Dinosaur Lady when he grows up—and he wants a mother and father of his own.

Matt Caldwell—He turned his cattle ranch into an unusual sort of "dude ranch"—one that specializes in horseback therapy for handicapped kids. That's how he knows Jason Reilly. And because of Jason's fossil find, he meets the dynamic Dr. Noelle Forrest, a.k.a. the Dinosaur Lady. He's definitely attracted, but he's got a problem with her, too. She wants permission to dig on his land and Matt's concerned this will disrupt his horses' routines. But he *might* be willing to compromise....

Dear Reader,

Kids—one minute you want to hug them, the next you want to strangle them! It's a wonder I'm not prematurely gray with some of the stunts my own two have pulled.

I'll never forget the time Andrew James, then only three, grew impatient while waiting for his father. He left my lap in the front passenger seat, slammed the gear lever of our idling car into Drive and proceeded to take me for a hair-raising ride in an icy winter parking lot!

Or the time my precocious daughter, Noel, felt the class field trip at Sea World moved too fast. She decided to conduct a more personal tour at her *own* speed. My phone call from the principal's office began with, "In twenty years of field trips, we've never lost a child—until yours."

But children can provide welcome surprises, too, like those offered by Jason Reilly. My Kids & Kisses character was modeled after two real-life children. The first was a little boy whose legs were forever being subjected to surgery, casts and therapy. He was so very brave, never crying during these painful procedures.

The second model I used was my son. I remember a terrifying moment eight years ago, when a speeding car squealed around the corner and headed straight toward Noel. From my kitchen window, I watched my two-year-old freeze at the edge of the curb. I screamed for her to move, knowing she couldn't hear me, knowing I couldn't reach her in time.

Then five-year-old Andrew raced toward her, grabbed her hair and yanked her to safety with mere inches, mere *seconds*, to spare. I ran outside, but Andrew already had Noel's hand and was walking her toward me. I must have been in shock, because I couldn't even hug them. I only stared and said, "Andrew, you just saved your sister's life."

He calmly replied, "I know."

Kids... One minute you want to hug them, the next you want to shake them. But as long as they're here to love, that's all that counts. This story is dedicated to children everywhere—especially my own two hellions, Noel and Andrew James. Hugs and kisses, kids!

Anne Marie Duquette

THE DINOSAUR LADY
Anne Marie Duquette

Harlequin Books

TORONTO • NEW YORK • LONDON
AMSTERDAM • PARIS • SYDNEY • HAMBURG
STOCKHOLM • ATHENS • TOKYO • MILAN
MADRID • WARSAW • BUDAPEST • AUCKLAND

ISBN 0-373-03328-1

THE DINOSAUR LADY

Copyright © 1994 by Anne Marie Duquette.

CHAPTER ONE

"FIVE MINUTES, DR. FORREST!" the assistant director warned. "It's my head if we run behind schedule today."

"I know, I know! I can't believe we're doing this *live,*" Noelle Forrest moaned as her makeup artist put the finishing touches on her face. "This is educational television, for heaven's sake, not Hollywood! We should be *taping* this, like we always do."

"We always go live during pledge week," the makeup artist said calmly. "You'll do fine, Noelle. It's not as if you didn't see this coming. After all, you've been with us for three years now."

"I know, but the last two years I wasn't part of pledge week. August came and went, and no one asked me to do a thing."

"Ah, but that's because your show wasn't as popular then as it is now. *Fun with Fossils* has really caught on. That's why the station manager wants you."

"But Woody knows I've never done *live* TV, Louise! I'm no actress—I'm a paleontologist. What if I make a mistake on camera?"

"Turn it into a joke." Louise put the last traces of blush below Noelle's nervous green eyes and patted her short mahogany hair. "After all, your viewers are young. They're an easy audience if you make them laugh. You're good with children. My kids love your show."

"Thanks." Noelle bit her lip. "I hope they still feel that way if I bomb."

Louise whipped off the white bib from Noelle's neck. "You won't. You never do."

"One minute, Dr. Forrest! Take your place, please!"

As Noelle rose to her feet, adjusting her classic skirt and blazer ensemble one last time, Louise gave her a fond maternal smile. "Break a leg, Noelle."

The background music began to play as the announcer's voice came on.

"Denver's Educational Station is proud to present *Fun with Fossils*. And your host for *Fun with Fossils* is Denver's very own Dinosaur Lady, Dr. Noelle Forrest!"

Noelle said a silent prayer that nothing would go wrong. Then she stepped into the glare of spotlights and the applause of the studio audience.

"Thank you for that warm welcome, boys and girls," Noelle said with a smile. "I'm Dr. Forrest, a paleontologist from the Colorado Museum of Paleontology. For those of you who are new with us today, I'll explain that a paleontologist works with ancient life-forms and fossil organisms. And as most of you know, my specialty is—"

She paused and let the children yell out, "Dinosaurs!"

Noelle smiled again. "That's right. Today we'll be talking about fossil deposits in our home state of Colorado. Thanks to our geology, we have the greatest number of dinosaur fossils in the nation. I'd like you all to learn exactly why. Here to help me with my presentation is today's guest host, Jason Reilly. He's eleven years old, and from Denver's local boys' club. Jason, please come down and join me."

All three cameras focused on the audience, but no child was rising excitedly to his feet.

Oh, no, Noelle groaned. Not stage fright! Not today of all days! Most children were eager to come up before the cameras, and of course her helpers were screened by the staff. There was the occasional child with cold feet, but then the producer merely stopped tape, changed children and resumed. The viewing public had never been the wiser—except this time.

"Jason, are you ready?" Noelle asked in her calmest on-camera voice.

"Just a minute," came the muffled reply. "I need to get my knapsack."

Noelle still couldn't locate her guest host. She took in a deep breath. "Perhaps Jason's club leader could give him a hand, and then point him out to our cameras?"

Noelle's taut nerves stretched even tighter as she saw that Jason was finally standing up and making his way down, complete with metal leg braces and aluminum crutches with arm bands. Dear Lord, her staff couldn't have known about the crutches or they would never have chosen this child.

"Jason, please be careful on the stairs," Noelle warned.

"Oh, I can do stairs easy," Jason said in a loud voice that the sound system easily picked up. "I've had lots of practice."

"So I see." Noelle watched as the towheaded boy wearing jeans, a *Jurassic Park* T-shirt and a knapsack negotiated the stairs with an ease that backed up his words.

Poor kid. I wonder how long he's been on those things?

"Wanna see me do two at a time?" the "poor kid" asked eagerly.

"No. I'm sure you'd have no problem, but let's stick with *one* at a time, please."

Noelle watched the boy with admiration—and concern. The stairs were one thing; the studio floor itself was covered with thick power cables. For safety's sake, she almost sent him back to his seat, live camera be damned. But there was an air of confidence about him that decided her against it. She settled for saying, "Jason, watch your footing. We have lots of cables you'll need to step over."

Jason nodded. He made it easily to her side, grinning widely, and Noelle breathed a huge sigh of relief.

"Hi, Dinosaur Lady! I mean, Dr. Forrest." Jason let go of the crutch handle and politely held out his hand to be shook.

"Hello, Jason. It's nice to meet you. Are you ready to help me with our talk?"

Jason's face fell. "I was hoping we could do the lab work first and the talk later."

The director gave Noelle a black look that said, "Hey, let's get this show on track." Noelle got the message and immediately set to work.

"Jason, have you watched my show before?" she asked.

"Oh, all the time!" He nodded vigorously, his head bobbing up and down.

"Then you know I lecture first and do the lab work second."

"I know." Jason gave her an angelic smile before stubbornly adding, "But I think we should skip the lecture today. I brought you a fossil."

"A fossil?" Noelle echoed, ignoring the director's growing frenzy.

"Yep," Jason said proudly. "Remember the show you did telling kids how to look for fossils?"

"I remember."

"Well, I found one. That's why I asked our club leader to bring us here—so I could show it to you. Do we have to wait until after the lecture?"

Noelle considered the boy carefully. It couldn't have been easy for him to search for fossils with those braces and crutches. Jason was one spunky kid, and she couldn't help responding to that.

"No, I guess we don't. Let's go over to my lab and check out this fossil of yours."

Jason gave her a big grin, while Noelle's director looked inches away from a heart attack. She knew what he must be thinking. There goes her script. There goes his *job* if Jason hurts himself—on *live* TV, no less. Here comes the first bad show in three years. There go all those pledges from viewers.

But suddenly Noelle didn't care. She was no actress worried about her acting career. And she wasn't about to wipe that eager look off the boy's face. She suspected Jason's "fossil" wasn't the real thing, but this was still a good opportunity to impart knowledge to her audience of young would-be paleontologists. She could always do the lecture later.

"Okay, young man, where's the fossil?" Noelle asked as they reached the left area of the studio set. She pulled out a chair for Jason, then sat beside him at the workbench holding her tools.

"It's in my knapsack." Jason dropped one crutch to the floor with a bang that had the sound man wincing. He twisted around to pull off his knapsack. "I did just what you said to do when I found it, Dinosaur Lady. I didn't try to scrape it clean."

Noelle nodded her approval. "You should never try to clean fossils yourselves," she told her audience. "They can be very fragile. What you might think is dirt and debris could actually be very important information. What should any paleontologist do next, Jason?"

Jason laid the knapsack on her workbench with much more caution than he'd used with his crutch. "You wrap the fossil in burlap, then plaster around it. Like this." The boy triumphantly brought forth his find.

"Very good," she said, noticing quite a professional plastering job. "Everyone, look closely at this." She held the plaster mass up for the cameras to zoom in on. "This protects the fossil from injury—"

"Until you can get it to an expert," Jason added, reciting her words by heart.

"You *have* watched my shows," Noelle said with a grin.

"Every one. Did I do it right?"

Noelle lowered the plaster-covered object back onto the workbench. "Oh, yes. Did you do this yourself, or did you have help?"

"I did it all myself. Well, someone mixed up the plaster for me. But he didn't put any on," Jason insisted.

"I almost hate to ruin it," Noelle said lightly, "but if we want to know what's inside, we'll have to crack it open. Jason, my tools, please."

By now Noelle had forgotten all about the show's being a live performance. Her students were totally enthralled with Jason's "fossil." Noelle sensed their fascination and suppressed a sigh. She was going to hate telling her audience that Jason's find was probably some dog's chewed-up bone. But that was paleontology for you.

She ought to know. *Those who can* discover, Noelle thought with envy. *Those who can't* study the existing finds—or talk about them for a living, like she did. But some day, somehow, she'd be one of those lucky ones. Jason was oblivious to her reverie. He was busily looking over the assortment of brushes, chisels, picks, hammers, magnifying glasses and small dentist's probes that were the tools of Noelle's trade. With great care he chose a small rubber mallet and a sharp-edged chisel.

"Will these do?" he asked with the confidence of a professional.

"They sure will."

"Don't forget your safety glasses," Jason added as he put on the spare pair. "We don't want any eye injuries."

This kid must have watched all her reruns, too, Noelle decided. "You're really very good, Jason," she said matter-of-factly. "I haven't had to tell you a thing yet."

Jason beamed, then threw his friends a gloating look. He certainly wasn't camera-shy.

"Now, if we can get a close-up here, I'll begin chipping away the plaster. You want to take it off gently so that the concussion of the hammer—the hammer blows—doesn't injure the fossil. Jason, why don't you tell everyone how you found this while I'm working?"

"Okay."

"Only please remember not to use last names or give out addresses, not even your parents'," Noelle cautioned as she put on her safety glasses.

"Foster parents," Jason corrected her. "I don't have real parents anymore."

Noelle paused, trying hard not to show her dismay on camera. Jason had certainly had his share of bad luck in life. The director glared at her, and she forced herself to regain her composure.

"You know we can't mention names on television without permission," she told him quickly.

He nodded. "Well, I was watching the show you did on kids finding fossils on our VCR. I have them all on tape, you know," Jason added. "I tape everything on dinosaurs. I even bought the book *Jurassic Park*, but I like your show better. It's more accurate than the movie. More interesting, too."

"I'm flattered." Noelle smiled as she started chipping. This boy was really some charmer.

"You said to look for fossils near cuts in the ground, like railroad tracks. Or quarries or riverbeds."

"That's right. Go on."

"Well, I go riding all the time, and I was looking."

Again Noelle stopped her work. "Not...bike riding?" she asked hesitantly.

"No, I can't do *that*. I go horseback riding out at the ranch. Matt's ranch. It's part of my therapy."

"No last names," she reminded him.

"I remember," Jason said good-naturedly. "Well, I was riding the creek-bed trail."

"Isn't that kind of dangerous?"

"No. It's dried up. Matt—he's in charge—uses it for the beginning riders. The gravel bottom makes horses go real slow. I'm not a beginner, but I wanted to check there for fossils. I was looking carefully, just like you told us, and I saw one."

"You could tell it was a fossil from up on horseback?" Noelle asked, surprised.

"Oh, yes. I've looked at lots of pictures of them, and it was lying right out in the open. I asked my therapist to get it for me. So she did."

Noelle resumed her work. "Your therapist was there with you?"

"Uh-huh. She walks next to the horse when I'm not with a group, in case I have problems. But I never do." Jason frowned. "I couldn't tell what kind of dinosaur the fossil was from, though. Neither could she."

Noelle's eyes sparkled with amusement. "It takes years of study to determine skeletal anatomy, Jason. And sometimes even paleontologists have a hard time identifying fossils. Don't feel bad. You did very well just to recognize this."

She finally reached burlap on one side of the irregularly sized plaster package. It looked as if the fossil itself was about five inches long.

"Well..." Jason didn't sound convinced. "I did what you said with the plaster as soon as I got home. I didn't want anything to happen—"

"Here we are—down to bare burlap!" Noelle announced. "Jason, would you like to peel away the cloth?"

"No, you'd better do it," he said in a serious voice. "You said the best place a fossil could be is with a professional. Oh, and in the hands of the public. Personal collections are so selfish, right?"

Noelle flushed. Her words sounded awfully preachy, but it was what she believed.

"That's right, Jason. Fossils belong in a museum where everyone can see and study them. It was very good of you to bring this to me." She carefully lifted a corner of the burlap.

"It's for you," Jason said proudly. "I want you to have it."

"Thank you, Jason. On behalf of the Colorado Museum of Paleontology, I accept," Noelle replied. "If, that is, this really is a bona fide fossil." She tried to prepare him for a letdown. "We can't be donating any old dog bones to the museum, now, can we?"

The audience laughed. Even Jason thought it was funny. "My foster parents have a dog," Jason said when the laughter died down. "But he wouldn't want this."

Noelle couldn't stall any longer. "Here goes," she said, slowly unwrapping the burlap. The cameras zoomed in and all the children in the audience held their breath. Noelle gasped. *It couldn't be.*

She removed her safety lenses with shaking hands, then snatched up a magnifying glass. Her trained eye took in the permineralized surface where the porous bone cavities had been filled with deposits. Her analytical mind reviewed modern animal skeletons versus ancient prehistoric structures, and compared them with this specimen. She hefted the solid remains, then carefully weighed it. Oblivious to everyone in the room, she grabbed for her pencil, notebook, ruler, and her brushes and probes. Her hands were everywhere; her mind was reeling.

It couldn't be! Or could it? This was a vertebrae, but a vertebrae larger than any commonly found on land. And it sure wasn't a whale vertebrae.

She suddenly became aware of someone calling her name.

"Dr. Forrest?" It was Jason. "Dr. Forrest, is everything all right?"

Noelle looked up at Jason. "Congratulations, Jason," she said in a hoarse voice. "You've made your first real dinosaur find."

The audience went wild. Jason's friends jumped up and down in their seats. The staff of *Fun with Fossils* stared frantically at Noelle, then at their scripts, then at Noelle again. For the first time on her show, Denver's Dinosaur Lady found herself at a loss for words.

The distraught director immediately gave Noelle the signal to go to break. Then gave it again. Noelle saw it the third time.

"We'll be back with Jason and *Fun with Fossils* in a moment," Noelle managed to say. "But first, these words on how you can help viewer-supported public television."

The camera's red light went off. Noelle reverently put down the fossil specimen and wiped her damp palms on her skirt. She ignored the director, ignored the audience, ignored everyone except Jason.

"I'd like your full name and address, Jason." Noelle grabbed her notebook and pencil. "For my records. You'll be in the history books on this one."

"Really?" Jason gasped.

"*Really.*"

"Can I come back on your show?"

"Count on it. And Jason, this man named Matt—the one who owns the ranch?"

"Yes?"

"Whoever he is, I *definitely* want to meet him."

JASON WAS WITH NOELLE in the car. All parents were supposed to pick up their boys at the studio after the show, but Jason's foster mother had called to say she'd been unavoid-

ably detained at Social Services. Jason was upset at hearing
he would have to go home with Mr. Jiminez, the boys' club
leader.

"I have a riding lesson today at Matt's! Can't you take me
there, Mr. Jimenez?" he'd begged.

But since the leader had to pick up his wife, he didn't have
the time for a lengthy detour. Noelle had offered to drop
Jason off at the ranch for his lesson. For one thing, she
couldn't wait to talk to Matt whatever-his-name-was about
conducting a dig on his land.

And if truth be told, there was something appealing about
Jason Reilly. It wasn't pity—although she hated to see any
child incapacitated. Nor was it his knowledge of paleontology, or his herolike worship of her "Dinosaur Lady" persona, flattering as that was. She'd simply enjoyed Jason's
company and welcomed the chance to know him better. He
tugged at her heartstrings in a way that her usual audience
of children never did. In fact, Jason evoked the same maternal feelings Noelle usually reserved for her sister Molly's
children. It was a surprising yet comfortable feeling.

Jason had been ecstatic at the suggestion that Noelle drive
him to his lesson. "You'd actually take me, Dr. Forrest?"

"Only if it's all right with your foster mother," Noelle
had replied. "And I have to talk to Matt—"

"Caldwell," Jason supplied.

"I have to talk to Mr. Caldwell, anyway."

Noelle made the phone call to Jason's foster mother herself. Mrs. Swanson had sounded hesitant at first, but Jason
had been determined and taken the phone line himself.

"She's not a stranger or anything, Mrs. Swanson," Jason said. "*Everyone* knows the Dinosaur Lady."

A few reassurances later, everything was set and she and
Jason were heading out to Matthew Caldwell's ranch together.

"Wouldn't it be neat if we found more fossils?" Jason
asked. "We could bring them on your show again!"

"These things take time, Jason. Dig sites can take
months, years." *If Mr. Caldwell even lets me look around,*
she thought. She'd have to make sure he did just that.

"I want to help," Jason insisted.

"You will, sweetheart. But not today. You have your riding lesson, remember?"

"I'd rather look for fossils with you."

"Jason, I promised Mrs. Swanson I'd get you safely to your lesson. I can't break that promise."

"I don't know why I have to listen to *her*," Jason grumbled. "She's not my *real* mother, you know."

"I know, but we both have to follow her instructions," Noelle said kindly. On a sudden urge, she ruffled Jason's hair. "Don't you worry, sweetheart. I'll keep you posted on all the latest fossil developments. I *promise.*"

Jason nodded, but he was still very quiet. Noelle decided to change the subject and get his mind off his disappointment.

"So tell me, Jason. How did you get started riding?"

The boy shrugged. "My social worker recommended horseback riding as part of my therapy."

"Physical therapy?"

"No, that's hospital stuff. Riding is *recreational* therapy. You know, for fun. Matt's ranch is for kids like me. They have therapists there to help us out."

Noelle nodded. "So Matt's the ranch owner, not a therapist?"

"He's both. Matt's the head therapist. There's others."

"Other therapists?

"Uh-huh. Three more. Two guys, plus one lady—Connie."

"Who takes care of the horses?" Noelle asked curiously. "Matt?"

"No, Matt's younger brother does. Alex is in charge of the ranch hands. Matt is in charge of the patients. They run the place together."

"I see." Noelle stopped at a red light. She took her eyes off the road to meet Jason's gaze. "Does the rest of Matt's family live on the ranch, too?"

"Nope. They're all dead."

"Dead?" she echoed.

"Yeah." Jason's voice was matter-of-fact. "In some accident."

"Oh, Jason..."

"They were out of town, and died on their way back home." Obviously this was old news, judging by Jason's manner. "Matt told me about them when I got upset about not having real parents to take care of me anymore. He said he understood. I think he really did." A warm glow appeared in Jason's eyes. "I like Matt."

"I can see that," Noelle said. She wondered what had happened to Jason's parents, but decided it wouldn't do to pry. The light changed to green. As she started the car again, she wondered what kind of man Matt Caldwell was. Apparently he was good with children, but she needed to know more about him than that.

"So, this Matt's a nice guy?"

"He's the greatest. He's a lot nicer than my assigned therapist," Jason sighed.

Noelle found herself worrying about the boy. "You don't like him?"

Jason shrugged. "It's a her. Connie's okay, I guess. But for a while she was more interested in Matt than she was in me."

"Connie is Matt's girlfriend?" Noelle blinked at the sudden change of subject.

"Not anymore. Alex didn't like Connie."

"Wait a minute, Jason, back up. Who's Alex again?"

"Alex is Matt's brother. He's out of town on a stock-buying trip—thank goodness."

Judging by Jason's wrinkled nose, Alex wasn't as popular as Matt. His next words confirmed it.

"Matt and Connie dated for a while. Alex didn't like it. He used to brag that he was the one who broke them up."

Noelle was incredulous. Why would anyone admit such an awful thing, and to a child, no less! "Alex really told you that, Jason?"

"Yes, but I don't believe him. Matt told me he and Connie just didn't work out, and Alex had nothing to do with it."

"You know, I really don't think this is any of our business," Noelle ventured to say. The conversation, especially the part about Alex, was making her very uncomfortable.

"Well, it's all over now. Matt and Connie are just friends. They don't kiss anymore like they used to. Yuck."

"Friends do kiss sometimes, Jason," Noelle said with an unexpected twinge of jealousy toward two people she'd never met. When was the last time *she'd* been kissed by a man? Unfortunately, in the male-dominated world of paleontology, competition instead of romance was usually the rule. Not that she succeeded at either very often, she thought ruefully.

Jason grimaced. "Well, Connie had better not try any of that mushy stuff on *me*," he said.

"I'm sure she's too busy with your riding lesson," Noelle assured him. "She's probably a very good therapist."

"She isn't interested in fossils. I practically had to beg her to get that fossil for me, you know, because she didn't believe me at first," he revealed disdainfully. "Only I didn't want to say that on TV."

"I'm glad you didn't. My director had enough on his hands. It isn't often we have a newly discovered fossil to unveil."

"What will happen to my fossil?"

"Well, I'll turn it in to the museum, and the staff will get to work on it right away."

"Why don't *you* get to work on it?"

Noelle sighed. The present status of her career was something she didn't particularly want to talk about.

"My boss has other plans for me," she said, her firm tone of voice decisively ending the discussion.

She *wasn't* happy about her present employer, or the way her career had stagnated. Her boss, Dr. Peabody, had made it clear he'd rather benefit from Noelle's free television publicity than any field or lab skills she might possess.

Unfortunately, Noelle couldn't just walk away. Paleontology jobs with any museum were few and far between. Most people, like herself, had to settle for what they could get. Her present employer was not her first choice. She'd wanted to work for the Denver Museum of Natural History, a top-rated museum that was internationally renowned for its Morrison Formation finds. But only the very best, highly credentialed and experienced paleontologists were offered positions there.

Noelle had to settle for a low paying, part-time position at the privately owned Colorado Museum of Paleontology. CMP was open to the public, but it was nowhere near as large or renowned as the Denver museum. However, any credible paleontologist needed museum affiliation, and right now, CMP was the best Noelle could do.

Unfortunately, affiliations and part-time hours didn't pay the rent. In desperation she'd applied for the job of host on the new educational TV show, *Fun with Fossils*. The producer had taken one look at her instant rapport with the test audience of children and hired Noelle on the spot. The extra money from her new job had taken the strain off her checkbook, but there had been an unexpected drawback.

Her show had become so popular that CMP directly benefited from the publicity. Her part-time museum position would never, ever materialize into the full-time, tenured position she wanted. CMP shamelessly advertised itself as "The Home of Denver's Dinosaur Lady," while offering Noelle nothing in the way of compensation. Noelle couldn't afford to quit *Fun with Fossils* until she had a full-time job at the museum, and the museum wasn't about to offer her one as long as CMP continued to get a free ride.

It was a no-win situation, leaving Noelle stuck between two worlds. She wasn't really a celebrity, nor was she an active paleontologist. It looked as though the only way she'd ever become fully tenured would be to break all ties with CMP and apply at another museum. The prestigious Denver Museum of Natural History was the only other game in town; applicants applied from all over the world for the rare openings that appeared.

Noelle knew that the Denver museum would never take her seriously, not while she taught "pop paleontology" to school children on a low-budget educational channel.

Unless she discovered the find of a lifetime, the find of the century....

Jason Reilly had put things in motion for her, but when it came to the big payoff, only time—and Matt Caldwell—would tell if she had a chance.

"Take a left, Dinosaur Lady!" Jason sang out. "We're here!"

CHAPTER TWO

NOELLE LOOKED UP and saw the neatly lettered sign nailed to a paddock fence. It read Caldwell Dude Ranch. Follow Arrows to Office.

Caldwell Dude Ranch. The place owned by Matt Caldwell. The place where, with any luck, she'd finally make a name for herself.

She drove the last stretch of gravel road, taking in the lush green paddocks, the horses and the carefully cultivated maple shade trees. To the west, the Rocky Mountains rose high and majestic, their jagged peaks softened by drifting clouds.

"Where do I drop you off? At the office?" Noelle asked as she reached the end of the road.

"Right here's good. There's Connie now."

Noelle saw an attractive young woman waiting at the head of a trail, the reins of a saddled mount in her hands. Noelle checked the car clock.

"You'd better hurry, Jason," she said as she parked her car in the lot with the others. "You don't want to keep your therapist waiting. Do you need any help getting out?"

"Nope, I can do it." Jason slung his backpack over his shoulders, slid his hands through the arm bands of his crutches and opened the door. "Thanks for the ride, Dinosaur Lady."

"You're very welcome, Jason."

Jason hesitated. "I gave you my phone number. You won't forget to tell me if you find any more fossils?"

"I have it, sweetheart. And I won't, I promise."

At that Jason flashed her a big grin, then headed toward his therapist. It wasn't until he was astride the horse that Noelle climbed out of the car. The heels of her pumps crunched on the gravel as she followed the arrows to first a paved sidewalk, then the office building itself.

She let herself in through the electric doors.

"Mom, look! It's the Dinosaur Lady!" one little girl immediately cried out. Squeals of delight filled the room, and Noelle found herself surrounded by a dozen children of all ages. She smiled and stayed perfectly still, afraid of upsetting the balance of those on crutches. Others in wheelchairs maneuvered in to get closer looks.

"It's not her," a few of the children argued.

"Is, too! Aren't you?"

"Yes, I'm the Dinosaur Lady," Noelle confirmed.

The noise level immediately jumped tenfold as the bolder children begged, "Can I come on your show?"

"No, me, let me! Please, please . . ."

"I wanna be on TV, too!"

There was only one thing to do. "If it's okay with your parents, you can all come down and see *Fun with Fossils,*" she announced. "I love having new faces in my audience."

Cheers and cries of, "Mommy, can I?" warred with, "But I wanna be *on* the show, not in the audience!"

The noise level rose to unprecedented heights as frustrated parents tried to calm eager children. Noelle had just decided to slip back outside when a door opened.

"What's going on out here?" came a deep voice.

The shouting immediately subsided.

"All of those standing, sit down. Those in wheelchairs, back against the wall. Hurry, please."

The voice wasn't loud. It wasn't even harsh. But the firm words had the desired effect. Noelle watched as every child in the room retreated to his or her previous position. Fascinated, she turned toward the new arrival as he spoke to the children.

"I'm trying to do an assessment with a patient, and I can't hear myself think. Let's keep it down, okay?"

A chorus of "Okay, Matt" and "Sorry, Matt" rang through the room. Matt gave them all a warm, approving smile.

"Now, what's going on out here?" he asked again.

Noelle's eyes were wide with surprise. She'd expected to see some white-coated, nondescript-looking, hospital-smelling therapist. The tall man before her looked like he'd stepped off a calendar of twelve prime male specimens, not like someone who'd be at home in a roomful of children. He wore jeans and a striped polo shirt; he had broad shoulders and a lean body. Despite Matthew Caldwell's size and vitality, there was a quiet grace in his movements.

The children didn't find him intimidating in the least, which was another surprise, since Noelle found his masculine presence more than a little intimidating. In fact, she found it compelling—something she wasn't pleased to admit. She was here to advance her career, she reminded herself, even as she continued to stare at the man.

Matt Caldwell's face revealed intelligence and humor, she noted. His sleeves were rolled to the elbows; his arms were tanned and muscular. Brown eyes, strong chin. The mouth was the only flaw in that handsome face. Right now it was pursed in a definite frown.

One of the older children spoke up. "It's the Dinosaur Lady, Matt. Don't you recognize her?"

"Ah, yes. Dr. Forrest." A sudden glimmer of recognition, and wariness, sparked in the dark eyes. "Mrs. Swanson told me you'd be dropping Jason off."

"Yes. I left him outside with his therapist. Connie, isn't it?"

"Then Jason's all set. Thanks for getting him here, Dr. Forrest. Now, if you'll excuse me..." Matt turned to leave.

"Oh, but wait! I wanted to talk to you about the fossil Jason found on your land."

Was it Noelle's imagination or was that a glint of anger in his eyes? Most people would be *excited* to hear about dinosaur fossils on their land. After all, this was Colorado, the fossil state.

"Sorry, Dr. Forrest. Today isn't a good day for drop-in visitors."

"I wasn't exactly a drop-in visitor. I was doing one of your patients a favor," Noelle calmly replied. *You aren't getting rid of me so easily,* she vowed. "But I certainly don't want to interrupt your work schedule. Perhaps I could make an appointment with your receptionist to see you later." Noelle glanced at the empty desk. "If she's on break, I can wait."

"She called in sick, and I have no one to replace her just yet. I can't spare any of my therapists." Matt's frown deepened. "I've got a call in for a temporary, but he won't be here until after lunch. Between covering the desk and doing my own work, I don't have time for visitors."

Noelle refused to take the hint, though Matt looked pointedly toward the door.

"I'm sorry to hear about your receptionist. Perhaps I could pitch in until the temp arrives? I could at least answer the phones and log in your patients."

"Thank you, no. I have everything under control, and I'd prefer not—" The phone rang. "Excuse me."

Noelle watched as Matt answered three successive calls that took up a good ten minutes of his time. When he finally hung up, he gave his watch a quick look that Noelle didn't miss.

"I really don't mind helping you out," she insisted. If it was a matter of finding fossils, she'd work for Attila the Hun if she had to.

Matt hesitated, and the phone rang again. He answered it, but this time put the caller on hold.

"I'll take you up on your offer after all, Dr. Forrest."

"Please, call me Noelle." She gave him her most engaging smile. To her secret dismay, she didn't see even the barest softening of his expression.

Apparently, Matt Caldwell was one tough customer. Well, when it came to her career, so was she!

"Show me what to do, Matt," she said.

His eyes narrowed at her use of his first name, but he refrained from comment.

"The log's here. You have to sign everyone in before they report for therapy. Children *must* be accompanied by an adult when going out to the stables. If their parents drop them off, that means you. If you're busy, here's the extension to the stables." He scribbled down a number. "Call and

have one of the therapists come down to the office. Any
questions, ask the patients. They know the routine."

A few more pointers, and Matthew Caldwell was gone.

The next hour was a harried one for Noelle. Paleontology was a slow, exacting, even delicate, business, and the
very things that made her a good paleontologist made her
an inferior receptionist. However, her people skills were
good, and she wasn't afraid to ask questions. Everyone was
only too happy to help out, especially those who recognized her as the Dinosaur Lady.

She logged in the group of children who were advanced
riders and got them out to their group class. She took care
of the patients with individual appointments. She answered
the phone, took concise messages and treated everyone with
courtesy. The frenzied morning rush tapered off as lunch
hour approached. It was with a sigh of relief that Noelle saw
only one patient, a young woman in a wheelchair, left in the
reception area.

"Can I help you?" she asked politely. She received a
morose look for her troubles.

"Not unless you can wave a magic wand and get me my
leg back."

"I'm sorry, but my receptionist's powers are rather limited," Noelle said briskly. "I *can* sign you in for your therapy appointment, however. If you'd give me your name,
please?"

The woman did, and Noelle logged her in.

"Do you need any help getting to the stables, or can you
manage on your own?"

"I can manage." The young woman gave Noelle another
unhappy look before the electric doors slid open, letting her
out of the room.

"You're very efficient, Dr. Forrest. Though perhaps a
little harsh."

Startled, Noelle looked up. She hadn't heard Matt open
the connecting door between his office and the reception
area.

"Maybe. But somehow I think pity would have gone
down a lot worse. Jason doesn't ask for it, and we seem to

get along just fine." She rose and picked up her purse. "Fortunately, that was the last patient of the morning," she told him. "The rest won't be here until after the temp shows up."

"Just for the record, you did the right thing," Matt admitted. "With the handicapped, you should never make extra allowances, except for those the handicap itself demands. Otherwise you treat them as you would anyone else."

"My sentiments exactly," Noelle replied. "Only. . ." She hesitated. "Don't you call them 'physically challenged?' "

"Handicapped is what they are, Dr. Forrest. My patients are handicapped by society. They're crippled by birth defects. Disabled by neglectful or abusive parents. Impaired due to the limits of modern medicine. Maimed by drunk drivers." His smile was chilly. "Your politically correct *physically challenged* doesn't begin to describe what my patients are—or what they must do to exist in a world that basically caters to survival of the fittest. Blunt honesty is more effective in helping my patients than fancy euphemisms."

"I'm glad you feel that way," Noelle replied. "I'm glad you prefer straight talk. It'll make what I have to say much easier."

"And that is?"

"I already know you have fossil-yielding land. If you have fossil-laden land, I want it."

There was an ominous silence. "I'm assuming that what you want is the fossils," Matt finally said, "because my land is not for sale."

"I can't get to one without the other. I want to dig, Mr. Caldwell. As soon as possible."

"No." Matt headed for the electric doors.

"No? Just like that, *no?*" Noelle hurried after him. "I deserve more of an answer than that!"

"Why?" he asked as they both stepped outside. "Because you helped me out of a tight spot this morning?"

"That'll do for starters." Matt's large strides forced her to step up her pace. "But mostly because dinosaur fossils are valuable finds. The knowledge they bring belongs to both the scientific community and the public. You know who I am, and you know what I do. Surely you don't expect me to simply walk away from a potentially fossil-rich area? All I'm asking is a few minutes of your time."

Matt sighed and slowed to a stop. "You're a very stubborn woman, Dr. Forrest. But I have work to do."

"Maybe we can talk while you show me around," she suggested. "I'd like to give your land a quick look-see."

"We're not going to trip over any old bones," he said sarcastically.

"You never know. I'll keep my eyes open just the same."

"It's a big place, and you can't cover it all on foot. Especially in those shoes." He gestured toward her dress pumps.

"Dinosaurs are big, too. I could spot an exposed fossil like Jason's in any shoes," she countered. "And I could always drive around your ranch."

"Sorry, my trails are for horses only. I don't suppose you ride?"

"I'm afraid I don't."

"Then you'd be in for a lot of walking. And as I said, my trails are for horses only."

Noelle reined in her temper. The man was being deliberately obstructive. "If I have to ride a horse to get a look at your land, I will." *There was no way she was giving up this easily!* "But I see no need. If I was on a horse, I'd be too high off the ground. I might miss something."

His eyes narrowed. "You're afraid of horses, aren't you?"

"Nervous, perhaps. They seem so big. But, as I said, if I have to learn to ride to use your trails, I'll learn to ride—no matter *how* big the horse is."

"The size of the horse or the rider has nothing to do with making a good equestrian team."

"You're deliberately changing the subject!" Noelle accused him. "I want to talk about organizing a dig here through my museum!"

"And I'm trying to show you why you can't. Now, follow me." Matt picked up his pace, taking her arm to steer her down the paved path. Noelle found that his warm touch distracted her from noticing the stables and all the activity taking place there.

In a few moments they were at the riding ring. "Here's my beginner class."

Noelle watched in amazement. "They're mostly children!" she marveled. "Look at them go!"

"As you can see, braces, crutches and missing limbs don't make any difference to them. They're just kids having fun."

Noelle nodded as she watched the instructor put the students and their mounts through different paces. Some even went over a few low jumps along the way.

"Incredible!"

"Not really incredible," Matt said. "Understandable. Think about it. Many of these children spend their whole lives in a wheelchair, except for a bed. Sitting on a horse gives them so much more freedom. You'd be eager to learn, too, if for no other reason than to break the monotony."

They walked closer. Noelle leaned against the fence, and Matt put one booted foot on the lowest rail, his hands loosely resting on the top. She ignored the neatly fenced paddocks with grazing horses to study his hands, instead. They were big, strong and callused, but she'd already felt how gentle they could be when he'd taken her arm. No wonder the children felt at ease with him.

Too bad the same couldn't be said for her....

"Even more mobile riders, like Jason Reilly, miss out on a lot. He can't do the normal things kids do, like pedaling a bike or going down a slide at a playground. But Jason can ride a horse, and that's something most of his friends *can't* do. Naturally he wants to excel. Look at him. He's the fourth horse from the leader."

"It *is* Jason!" Noelle watched as Jason expertly followed the instructor's orders. "But you said this is a beginner's class. Jason told me he wasn't a beginning rider."

"Children tend to brag."

Noelle continued to watch in amazement. The little boy was full of surprises. So, it appeared, was the ranch owner. "How does he keep from falling off?"

"We alter the tack. My brother is a talented leathersmith. He can usually come up with some kind of leg rig or harness to compensate for limited muscle strength."

"You must mean Alex."

Matt studied her for a moment. "You know about Alex?"

"Jason mentioned his name. And that you were a recreational therapist, not a physical therapist."

"Jason's quite the little chatterbox," Matt said, but the warmth in his eyes at Jason's name took the sting from his words. "There isn't much he misses."

Noelle was intensely aware that not one thing she'd said or done so far had brought a similar softness to Matt Caldwell's expression.

"How did you get interested in recreation therapy?" she asked.

"I like being outdoors," he said. "A physical therapist usually works in a hospital setting. A recreational therapist doesn't. I don't know if Jason mentioned it, but Alex was the first special patient I taught to ride."

"No... no, he didn't."

"Alex was in an accident—the same accident that killed our parents. His injuries were quite extensive, and not completely reversible," he told her in a quiet voice. "Hence my choice of jobs. Plus I felt that being a recreational therapist worked better with the family ranch business. I could work at home."

"You were originally a horse rancher?"

"No. A cattle rancher. Alex and I switched over to the dude ranch business some time ago."

"That's some career change," Noelle said curiously. "It must have been hard for both of you... especially Alex."

"Yes, it was."

Something in the way he said it let Noelle know that any other questions wouldn't be welcome. She went back to watching Jason ride.

"So, do the children live here, or do they come and ride whenever they want?"

"Neither. We try for something in between the two. I work out a schedule that meets their own particular abilities and needs, then expect them to adhere to it."

"Kind of like taking piano lessons?"

"Kind of." Matt smiled. It was the first real smile she'd seen from him, one that actually reached his eyes. She was surprised at the difference it made. He went from being simply attractive to dangerously magnetic. "I think of these boys and girls as healthy children taking riding lessons, and doing pleasure riding on a regular basis."

"Why aren't there more places like this?" Noelle asked curiously. "Places catering to people like Jason Reilly?"

"The usual reason—money," was the blunt answer.

Matt took her arm again, and they started toward the stables area.

"Private insurance companies aren't willing to spend money *entertaining* people, as they call it." Matt's lips curled derisively. "They'll cover physical therapy costs, but most balk at recreational therapy."

"I find that hard to believe."

"It's true, though. If medical insurance companies subsidized places like mine, there'd be hundreds of them across the country. Unfortunately, there aren't, and only the well-off can afford the few that do exist. I try to take on as many needy cases as I can, but that's not a whole lot," he admitted. "I have to pay my therapists' salaries and feed the animals, and I can't do that without charging."

"What a shame!"

"It certainly is. The United States is one of the wealthiest nations in the world, but we have no comprehensive national health plan. It's a crime that people have to pay so dearly for medical treatment. To make matters worse, the more medical problems you have, the less likely you'll find an insurance company willing to underwrite you. It's a vicious circle. The people who really need it, like those children you saw, are the ones least likely to find adequate coverage. Unless their parents have money, they're out of luck."

"It doesn't seem right."

"It isn't. That's why I'm involved with a group that's been lobbying Congress for a national health care system. So far there's been a lot of talk about legislation, but not much else."

"I had no idea...."

"Most people don't. That's a major part of the problem. And speaking of problems, yours still remains, Dinosaur Lady."

Noelle blinked at the sudden change of subject.

"I know why you're here and I know what you want. However, I've made my decision. You're not going to dig up my land."

"But why not?"

Matt stopped just outside the stables; his guiding hand on her arm falling to his side.

"You come in with your bulldozers and backhoes, Dinosaur Lady, and my patients' safety goes right out the window."

CHAPTER THREE

"BULLDOZERS AND BACKHOES?" Noelle couldn't believe her ears.

"First of all, Mr. Caldwell, paleontologists rarely use bulldozers and backhoes. Picks and shovels are the usual tools of our trade. And if you think I'm here to trample over innocent children on my way to the fossil beds, you're wrong!"

"Am I?" he asked calmly, not at all affected by her outburst.

"Yes, you are!" Her cheeks flushed an angry red as she fought to control her temper. "You know, you're about as subtle as a bulldozer yourself!"

"I have good reason. Follow me," he ordered.

She allowed herself to be led inside the stable to the nearest stall.

"You see these horses?" He rubbed a velvet muzzle. "I have to specially train them for my riders. They're gentle, dependable and they don't spook easily. Most important, they live a life of strict routine. Same trails, same times, same gaits."

Noelle looked at the other horses curiously watching from their stalls. "It sounds rather boring," she said, her words curt and clipped.

"Perhaps. However, horses who know what's expected of them are safe horses. They aren't going to throw an inexperienced rider with braces or prosthesis or other hardware. My mounts are like old plow horses. They know the routine, and nothing distracts them. *Almost* nothing, that is."

"What are you saying, Mr. Caldwell? That I'd be a disruptive influence on your ranch?"

"Exactly, Dinosaur Lady."

He'd practically thrown the name in her face. And she had a gut feeling the Dinosaur Lady was in for some bad news. She was right.

"If you go digging up my land for fossils, you destroy my horse trails. Or my riding rings. Or my paddocks. And that means changes. This ranch can't afford changes. My horses are exceptionally calm because they don't deal with the unexpected."

His hand dropped from the horse's head as he quietly turned to face her.

"I'm sure your intentions are good, Dr. Forrest. I grew up in Colorado, and I know how valuable fossils are. I'm afraid I just don't consider them as valuable as my children."

"And you don't think I feel the *same?*"

Matt hesitated, as if searching for a polite way to reply. "Since I don't know you well, I really can't say. I *can* say that I don't intend to take any chances when it comes to this ranch. Not with you. Not with anyone."

Noelle drew in a deep breath. "Just how can I prove to you that you *wouldn't* be risking anything with me?"

"You can't."

The answer was blunt, but Noelle still refused to give up hope.

"Oh, but I can." She just had to figure out how, and she was running out of time, even as Matt was running out of patience.

"Dr. Forrest, please. I'm short-handed, and I've wasted enough time today—time I don't have to spare."

"I can take a hint, Mr. Caldwell. You want me to leave."

Matt didn't try to dissuade her. "I'm sorry to refuse your request to dig, but you have to understand the position I'm in."

"I do understand your position." A sudden brilliant idea flashed in her mind, and she gave him her sweetest smile. "Now let me explain mine."

"Yes?" They stepped out of the stable into the sunlight.

"I'm a very influential person. I'm well-known with the media, and more important, the public. And this week is pledge week at my station. It's amazing how many potential sponsors and patrons I run into. The money they have..." She shook her head for emphasis. "It's amazing. The station could do your ranch a lot of good financially. *I* could do your ranch a lot of good financially. Did you ever think of that?"

She watched as his face flooded with realization.

"I can see you haven't," she said, enjoying his reaction. "Maybe you should. Think of all those needy children without insurance who'd love to come to your ranch. I'm more than willing to help, Mr. Caldwell."

"For a price?" The words were spoken through gritted teeth.

"For a compromise," Noelle corrected him. "You scratch my back, I'll scratch yours. Isn't that how the saying goes?"

Matt's eyes narrowed with contempt. "You'd use my patients—innocent children—just to further your own career?"

Noelle felt her blood pressure rise, but she hadn't spent years working in a male-dominated profession, not to mention the frantic world of television, for nothing.

"Don't throw my career in my face, Mr. Caldwell. Children pay *both* our salaries. Business is business. I'd bet my last fossil probe you cash your checks just like I cash mine," she countered. "Or am I wrong?"

Matt's furious expression told Noelle she wasn't.

"I thought so. And while we're on the subject of children, Mr. Caldwell, how about what you're doing to Jason?"

"Just what are you talking about?"

"Jason is more than some juvenile charmer. He has a maturity and intellect well beyond most kids his age. His knowledge of paleontology impresses me, and I don't impress easily. Don't you see? Jason is gifted! Well and truly gifted! I can't believe you'd deny Jason Reilly—and the rest of my 'Fun with Fossils' kids—the opportunity to learn about a fossil dig firsthand."

"This isn't about the kids!"

"You're probably right." Noelle studied him carefully. "It *isn't* about children. It's all about your bank account. An influential visitor offers to get you plenty of donations, and you practically throw her off the ranch. You don't have a very good head for business, do you?"

Matt's fists clenched at the insult, but Noelle went on.

"*Now* I understand why you can't take on any more needy patients, Mr. Caldwell. You're only interested in teaching *rich* children how to ride. After all, there's no profit in charity, is there?"

There was a moment of silence. Then, "If you weren't a woman, Dinosaur Lady, I'd have you facedown in the dirt right now."

"To leave my bones for my colleagues?" she retorted, her eyes just as cold as his. "I might be forced to return the favor. Then maybe the next time a perfectly legitimate business proposition comes your way, you'll be less free with the insults. Just what kind of fossil-hungry monster do you think I am?"

She spun on the ball of her foot, not giving him a chance to answer. "Don't bother showing me to the car," she said, tossing the words over her shoulder. "I can find my own way. If you change your mind and want to do business, give the studio a call. We're in the book."

"Don't count on it," she heard him say, but Noelle refused to give him the satisfaction of reacting.

As if she'd ever deliberately ruin the work he was doing with those children! She was so angry she could barely concentrate on driving. But her anger soon faded when she realized that one fact remained. She, Noelle Forrest, held potentially valuable purse strings to help those special children and their special horses. Sooner or later, Matt Caldwell would change his mind—and she'd better be prepared when he did.

By the time Noelle was back inside her apartment, she'd completely calmed down. As she discarded the skirt and blazer, she tried to reevaluate the situation from Matt's point of view.

A locally well-known and obviously ambitious paleontologist shows up at his ranch, claiming fossils could exist beneath his horse trails. Of course he felt threatened. No, he felt that his *patients* were threatened. Matt was like a fierce lioness protecting her cub. Or rather, she thought, remembering that vivid male vitality, an angry lord of the jungle.

Still, there was such a thing as going overboard, she reflected as she slipped into some casual clothes. Lofty ideals were wonderful, but they wouldn't pay her rent any more than they'd pay for would-be riders without health insurance.

But Noelle was hopeful. She might not be heaven's gift to men—in fact, considering the male prejudice at CMP, she didn't want to be. However, with children, Noelle had a sharp maternal instinct that seemed to have kicked in when she met Jason Reilly. If the boy claimed Matt was "a great guy," then she was prepared to accept those words at face value. Matt would definitely look out for his patients' best interests.

Noelle felt positive there was more to Matt Caldwell than what she'd seen today. She'd just have to play the waiting game. After all, she'd been doing it her whole career. Why should this be any different?

Trust another man to make life difficult for me. And wouldn't you know he'd have to be intelligent, great with kids, and good-looking to boot. She sighed, then caught herself. *Think positive,* she scolded her flagging spirits. *Concentrate on the fossils.* Matt Caldwell would come around. In the meantime, she should be planning her campaign to get back on his ranch, shovel in hand. Tonight, she'd work on putting together a list of sponsors.

Right now, though, she needed a breather. She sat down at her desk, turned on the answering machine, then picked up her waiting mail and thumbed through it.

Beep. "Hi, sis. It's Molly."

Noelle smiled as her younger sister's voice came on the line. She was lucky that both her parents and her only sibling lived fairly close.

"What's the scoop? Are we still on for the family barbecue next weekend? Mom and Dad said you didn't have to work, and the kids are expecting you. Call me later, okay? Bye."

The machine beeped a second time.

"Hello, Dinosaur Lady. This is the studio."

Noelle groaned aloud. The staff of *Fun with Fossils* never called her at home unless there was trouble.

"I know you were supposed to have the next two days off, but we're moving next week's show up to tomorrow. The station got tons of pledges during your last show, so we're going live again. Sorry, Dr. Forrest. See you at 9:00 a.m. sharp."

"Not live again!" Noelle groaned. She had enough on her mind already without another live show. She rubbed her temples and debated getting some aspirin. This was turning out to be one exasperating day.

The machine beeped a final time.

"Dr. Forrest? This is Matt Caldwell."

Noelle sat up straight in her chair, the pile of mail forgotten. How had he obtained her private number? And so quickly? Once she'd become the Dinosaur Lady, she'd been forced to get an unlisted number to prevent frequent calls from adoring children. Very few people had that number.

"I'd like to see you again."

Her heart quickened with excitement. "So would I, Mr. Caldwell," she said aloud. "For more reasons than one."

"Please call me so we can set up a time," the message continued. "You have my office number, but feel free to use my home phone after hours." He carefully gave the latter twice, and she jotted it down. "Hope to hear from you soon. Goodbye."

The answering machine clicked, then rewound.

Noelle sat there with a grin on her face, the sound of his voice still echoing in her head. Mr. Caldwell had certainly undergone a rapid change of heart. She'd bet her last fossil probe he wanted her help in getting sponsors. Amazing what changes the almighty dollar could produce. He'd gone from the lordly protector to the polite supplicant.

Still, Noelle couldn't work up any real anger over that. She certainly would have done the same thing in his place. After all, it was for a good cause. Too bad Matt had become interested in her only *after* he'd realized her monetary value. Not once had he looked at her with a gleam of male appreciation in his eyes. Not that she was searching for romance, but still, it was disappointing. Even a bit...insulting.

Noelle pushed that thought away and reached for the phone. Then she paused.

Matt Caldwell's disdainful looks, his temper and, worst of all, his accusations, had hurt. Somehow he'd penetrated that tough, almost cynical barrier she'd used to protect herself against the male slings and arrows of her world. Her hand hovered over the phone, then retreated. She defiantly lifted her chin.

Let him sweat it out a bit, she decided. She'd show him that—despite her love for children—Dr. Noelle Forrest was no pushover. She went back to her desk and turned on her computer. Working as she did for a small, viewer-supported educational station, she knew a fair number of the big sponsors. She also knew the ones who might be interested in privately donating to a project like Matt's. She'd print him out a list of names and addresses.

No matter what she'd told Matthew Caldwell, no matter how low the man thought she would go, Noelle intended to do the right thing. Even if he ultimately refused to let her dig, she'd get him both sponsors and donations for his ranch.

Of course, the high-and-mighty Mr. Caldwell didn't have to know that, she thought with satisfaction. She had the world's best poker face, thanks to her boss, Dr. Peabody, and all the other paleontologists at CMP who'd kept her career off the fast track—because they considered her more valuable as a source of free advertising than as a professional like themselves. But Matt didn't need to know *that,* either. If he wanted to sponsor more needy children, he'd have to come to her. And perhaps *then* he'd allow her to dig on his ranch.

So what if he wasn't interested in her as a woman? She had a strong ego. Besides, her career was on the line. She'd just have to concentrate harder on finding more fossil specimens.

Despite the fact that she found Matt Caldwell a very enigmatic specimen indeed....

"I DON'T KNOW HOW you expect me to finish your makeup if you keep frowning," Louise complained.

"Sorry." Noelle relaxed her face. "Better?"

"You'll scare those kids away if you go on the show looking like that," Louise replied, dusting blush on Noelle's cheeks. "I haven't seen you like this since you broke up with your last gentleman friend."

"He was no gentleman, and that's why I got rid of him," Noelle said with an amused smile. "But yes, it's a man who's got me upset."

Louise nodded. "That's good news—about the man, I mean. When you're still single at your age—"

"Thirty-one is hardly old!"

"You can't wait forever."

"Now you sound like my mother," Noelle grumbled. "And for your information, this man is a business contact, not anyone I've dated."

"But you'd like to?"

"It'd be kind of hard, since all he's interested in is my sponsor contacts," Noelle muttered, feeling for the envelope in her blazer jacket. She was unaware that she'd revealed her interest in Matt until she saw Louise's smug look in the mirror.

Noelle realized she'd been trapped. "You know something, Louise? If you weren't such a good makeup artist, I might have to request a replacement."

"As if you could. This is educational TV," Louise said with a laugh. "I'm it. And even if this were the networks, you wouldn't. You're too nice."

"Great. Men don't like *nice* women nowadays. Ask my last few dates. I've given up finding Mr. Right."

Louise took off the makeup bib. "The kids like you, even if the men don't."

"Gee, *thanks,* Louise. I feel *much* better now."

"Dr. Forrest, five minutes!" yelled a *Fun with Fossils* staff member. "Remember, we're going live again!"

"As if I could forget."

"Break a leg," the makeup artist called after her. "And for heaven's sake, don't forget to smile."

"Yeah, right," Noelle groaned. She adjusted her blazer, clipped the microphone over her pocket and stepped out into the bright, blinding lights.

"Six seconds. Five, four—" The director counted off the seconds on his fingers, then silently pointed toward her on "one." The background music began to play as the announcer's voice came on with the familiar introduction.

"Denver's Educational Station is proud to present *Fun with Fossils.* And your host for *Fun with Fossils* is Denver's very own Dinosaur Lady, Dr. Noelle Forrest!"

The kids cheered, and Noelle felt some of her despondency leave at their warmth. The audience was mostly six-year-olds, an age group Noelle especially loved to work with. They were old enough to be interested in science, and young enough to get wildly enthusiastic over learning.

Best of all, Jason Reilly was there again, this time with his foster mother. He waved excitedly, trying to attract Noelle's attention. She felt more of her gloom disappear. What a special little guy he was. Not only was he one heck of a smart kid, he had a heart-stopper of a smile. Braces or no braces, how could his mother ever have given him up? Noelle threw him a brilliant smile to let him know she'd seen him. Jason's returning grin chased away the rest of her bad mood.

With a sense of genuine enjoyment, Noelle introduced the day's program, the one Jason's fossil had preempted yesterday. In fact, the show would have gone perfectly if Jason was up there on stage. Her little helpers usually made her job more difficult; Jason had been an exception.

Perhaps she'd think about asking him back again. In the meantime, she had a show to do. She was pleased to see that the children were eager to learn why their home state had more fossils than anywhere else.

"If we can turn up the studio lights, I'll bring down my guest helper for today," Noelle announced.

The lucky young girl sprang to her feet, and the cameras focused on her. Noelle smiled, then froze. The lights showed rows of shining young faces. They also showed the face of Matt Caldwell. He was sitting so far back in the audience, Noelle doubted even Jason had noticed his appearance yet.

But *she* certainly had. Noelle's professional calm almost deserted her. She was dying to know what he'd decided, dying to know if her career actually had a chance. She had to force herself to concentrate on her script—and to keep from stealing glances at him.

It was a relief to go to their first pledge break.

"We'll return with *Fun with Fossils* right after this," she announced. Noelle motioned for a staff member as soon as they were off the air. "I'll be right back," she said to her guest. "Bill, watch my little helper for me. I see someone in the audience I need to speak to."

"Sure thing, Dr. Forrest. Only make it quick. This is live, you know."

Noelle merely nodded. "Here, hold this, please." She took off her mike, then strode purposefully toward Matt Caldwell. She was glad he was sitting away from the main group, out of earshot of the children. So far, their conversations hadn't been the type she'd want to broadcast.

Matt looked up expectantly as she approached. "Dr. Forrest" was his not-very-warm welcome.

"Mr. Caldwell. I'm surprised to see you here," she remarked. "Don't you have patients scheduled? I thought you'd be at work."

"I would be if you'd returned my call." His eyes were accusing. "Since you didn't, I had to leave my ranch to track you down. So now we're a therapist short. I'm sure you received my message."

"I did," she admitted. "However, I was working last night." That much was true. It had taken her all evening to assemble the list of sponsors, and she still wasn't finished.

"If you remember, I asked you to call me at the studio. If I'd wanted to talk to you last night, I would have given you my home number. My *unlisted* number," she emphasized. "Just how did you get it, anyway?"

"I called the front desk and told them who I was."

"They usually know better than to give out my number." Noelle tried to convey her disapproval, but it was hard. The man was certainly resourceful. Too bad his reasons for wanting to contact her were professional and not personal, she thought suddenly. With an effort she hid her dismay. "You must have been quite convincing, Mr. Caldwell."

"I was. I wanted to speak to you right away."

"About these?" Noelle reached into her jacket pocket and withdrew her envelope. "The names?"

"You know the answer to that." Matt started to reach for the envelope, but Noelle immediately slipped it back inside her pocket.

"I don't think so, Mr. Caldwell. We have some serious talking to do."

"I can't wait around here all day!" Matt spat out.

"Then you should have followed my instructions, called the studio and made an appointment," she retorted.

The director yelled out her name and motioned for her to get back onstage.

"As you can see, Mr. Caldwell, you're not the only person too busy to see drop-ins," she couldn't resist adding.

"Dr. Forrest, you're on in twenty seconds!"

Noelle raised her eyebrows. "If you'll excuse me, duty calls." She hurried back to her station and finished clipping the microphone back onto her blazer just in time.

Saved by the bell, Noelle thought with satisfaction. Matt looked ready to explode, but he didn't leave. It appeared there were some benefits to live TV, after all.

"Hello, boys and girls. We're back with *Fun with Fossils.* As you remember, we were discussing the geography of Colorado. It's the Rocky Mountains that make our state such a special place for finding dinosaur bones."

Out of the corner of her eye, she saw Matt cross his arms.

"Parts of Colorado's Rocky Mountains date back to prehistoric times. While many mountain ranges are quite new, ours are very old. Dinosaurs actually roamed our state near Pike's Peak and the Red Rocks area."

She could see Matt and patted her blazer over the inside pocket. An angry expression crossed his face as Noelle pretended to smooth her lapels. Oh, yes, she had him right where she wanted him.

Goodbye, Dr. Peabody. Goodbye, Colorado Museum of Paleontology. Goodbye *Fun with Fossils.* But instead of triumph, Noelle felt a strange pang. Funny how that last realization conjured up such a feeling of regret. She looked into the audience at the many young faces and deliberately made a silly play on words. They all burst into laughter. For a moment her resolution wavered. How could she give this— give *them* up?

Be sensible, she scolded herself. Those children all had their own parents, their own families to go home to. She was just a temporary diversion; she made no more difference in their lives than an afternoon cartoon on TV or a cheap comic book from the drugstore. In fact, that was all the Dinosaur Lady really was—a sort of cartoon character who existed only for the free museum publicity and station pledges she could drum up. The children might not know the difference yet, but she certainly did.

The fossil digs were where she could *really* make a difference, Noelle told herself. It was best to get this silly sentimentality about would-be paleontologists out of her mind. They liked her, but they didn't *need* her. It wouldn't do to get too attached to being the Dinosaur Lady. Or to the children from the schools and the Scout troops and the boys' and girls' clubs. For all she knew, they could have been dragged down, full of protests, to see her show.

Although they seemed to have a good time once they were here, a voice whispered. Noelle ignored it and busied herself with her presentation.

Her little helper lifted a face full of worshipful awe as Noelle handed her the pointer to use on the map. Noelle felt a tinge of guilt, then forced herself to look away from the little girl and out into the audience. Jason Reilly enthusiastically waved to her again.

A strange, sad feeling fluttered inside her, but she refused to give in to it. Refused to even acknowledge it.

Concentrate on your real *career,* she told herself. *Just think of Matt's ranch, and how you can't wait to get your hands into his soil. You've been passed over by men without your qualifications, knowledge or experience for three years. Don't go soft now, or you'll be stuck doing* Fun with Fossils *until you're old and gray.*

She stiffened, if not her resolve, then at least her backbone. She paused for a moment, looked Matt right in the eye, then continued her lecture.

"Our geological formations also help us find fossils. Colorado is lucky enough to have one called the Morrison Formation. It's a layer of rocks extremely rich in dinosaur fossils. Most major finds in our state come from this layer. The Morrison Formation is shale and sandstone that was deposited here in Jurassic time. Who can tell me how many million years ago that was?" she asked, pointing to the time chart.

"One hundred and sixty!" most of the children shouted out. Jason, she couldn't help but notice, was the loudest of all.

"That's right," Noelle replied. "The Morrison Formation was originally a broad floodplain with lots of vegetation and slow-moving streams, perfect for preserving fossils."

She watched as Matt stood and headed for the exit. For a moment she nearly panicked. Had he guessed she was bluffing? Was he calling her bluff even now? Noelle swallowed hard.

"Now, if my helper would come with me to our map, she and I will show you where some of Colorado's more recent finds have been made."

The little girl stood up, but Noelle's mind was on Matt. She'd track him down later, she vowed, and went on with her talk.

"We've made some important discoveries in Grand Junction," she began, slipping into her prepared speech.

Finally the half hour was over. Noelle made her closing remarks, the children clapped, her little guest host gave her a big hug, and the red lights on the cameras finally went off.

Noelle gave a big sigh of relief. She wanted only to rush off, to find Matt. But she stayed a few extra minutes to talk to the children, sign a few autographs and introduce herself to the adults. Eventually, however, the children headed back to their buses or rides in the parking lot.

Jason then eagerly introduced her to his foster mother.

"Hello, Mrs. Swanson." Noelle was interested in meeting the woman but had to hide her impatience. At this rate it would be too late to hurry out into the main corridor to look for Matt. "I'm very pleased to meet you."

"Jason's told me so much about you," Mrs. Swanson said. "He just adores your show. I can't believe how much he's learned from it. We may have a budding paleontologist on our hands."

Jason beamed, and then proceeded to ask Noelle question after question. By the time she'd satisfied his curiosity and farewells were said, a good half hour had gone by. So much for finding Matt. She'd have to change tactics.

"Great show!" Louise called out as Noelle headed out. She'd just left her dressing room after washing off the heavy studio makeup and changing into casual slacks. "Woody's really pleased with all the pledges you're getting. He says we'll have to go live more often."

Noelle grimaced. Woody was a great station manager, but he didn't always make her life easy. "Please, don't encourage him!" she called back. She didn't break stride, intent on hurrying to the parking garage.

"Oh, wait!" Louise shouted after her. "There's someone waiting for you in the front lobby."

Her pulse sped up with excitement. "Who?"

"A Mr. Caldwell."

"Thanks, Louise. I'll see you later." Noelle made her way to the main elevator. She stepped inside, laden down with her purse and dress clothes in their plastic bag. When it stopped at the main floor, Noelle forced herself not to hurry out. No need to appear too eager.

"Waiting for someone, Mr. Caldwell?" she asked as she approached the seating arrangement marked Visitors.

He rose to his feet. "You know damn well I am—and why."

"Do I? You didn't stay for the whole show," she snapped, then could have kicked herself for the remark. It sounded as if she had a bruised ego. Still, he could have shown *some* interest in *Fun with Fossils*.

"I know Jason would have liked to say hello," she added.

"I talked to Jason and Mrs. Swanson a few minutes ago," he said tersely. "Now, if you don't mind, is there someplace we can talk in private?"

"You can walk me out to my car," she replied. "The parking garage is right across the street."

A few minutes later they'd arrived. She unlocked her door and laid her clothes on the passenger seat, then turned to face him. It was time to negotiate.

Obviously Matt thought the same thing. "Are we ready to deal?" he asked grimly.

Noelle couldn't help smiling.

"You find this amusing, Dr. Forrest?"

"It is kind of funny," she said. "Here we are in a dark parking garage to do a deal. It's a little clichéd, don't you think?"

"Would you prefer a candlelit table with singing violins instead?"

The smile faded from her face, but not because of Matt's obvious sarcasm. Suddenly she found herself *wanting* to sit at a candlelit table with him. He was the first man she'd been attracted to in a long, long time. And as if that unsettling realization wasn't bad enough, she had to deal with the fact that all *he* wanted to do was get down to business.

"Here's the deal," he said. "You give me that list of names, and I give you one week to dig on my ranch."

"One week!" Noelle exploded. "It might as well be one second! What do you expect me to do in one week?"

"Whatever it is you paleontologists do. Pound stakes. Dig dirt. Take photos. Whatever." He folded his arms across his chest. "One week. That's all I'm willing to give you."

"Forget it. I find your deal quite...unacceptable." She opened the car door. "If you'll excuse me, you're wasting *my* time."

She climbed into her car and slammed the door. It was immediately opened again.

"If you want to search my ranch for fossils, Dr. Forrest, you'll reconsider."

"I can't search for fossils in one week." She defiantly inserted her key into the ignition. "Get away from my car."

Matt reached inside and yanked her keys out of the ignition. Noelle made no attempt to grab them back.

"Save the strong-arm tactics for your horses," she said coldly, "because I'm not impressed."

"One week," Matt repeated.

"Sorry, Mr. Caldwell. No sale. Now give me my keys."

"One week, and I let you stay on the ranch for the whole time."

Noelle met his eyes. "I'm listening."

"You'll have as much freedom as I can allow you during the day."

"And when the riders are gone?"

"Complete freedom after hours."

Noelle considered his proposition. Once pledge week was over and the studio was back to taped shows, she'd be able to get the time off. As for the museum, that would be no problem. They never gave her any real work, anyway. But still...

"No," she announced.

"No?"

"One week isn't long enough. I want two."

His eyebrows rushed together. "One and a half."

"Two or no dice."

Matt started to say something, then stopped and gave her a dangerous smile. Noelle didn't like that look one bit.

"Two weeks, and you handle all the sponsors. *You* write the letters. *You* do the follow-up phone calls."

"That's a heck of a lot of work!" she protested. "Are you going to help?"

His smile grew. It reminded her of a fairy-tale wolf's smile. All teeth, no real friendliness. "Nope. I'll just sit back and wait for the money to roll in."

Damn! He'd maneuvered her right into a corner. But Noelle wasn't finished yet. "Two weeks, I handle the sponsor work, *and* I get an assistant of my choosing."

"To help you with the pledge work?"

"No, to help me at the dig site."

"Forget it."

"Forget it?" she echoed.

"Forget it. As in no way. Don't hold your breath. Don't count your prehistoric chickens."

"I get the message, so skip the sarcasm," Noelle retorted. "I want to know why I can't have an assistant. It's a logical request."

"Why? Having one of you hovering around disturbing my patients and my horses is bad enough."

Noelle took in an indignant breath. "You can't expect me to do all the work with the sponsors *and* try to pin down a possible dig site myself!"

"You'll have to manage somehow," came the infuriating response. "Because I'm not changing my mind on this. And there's more. Thanks to your show, Jason's find is no secret. Fortunately no one's connected it with my ranch yet. I intend to keep it that way. I don't need a slew of paleontologists or media swarming all over my land. If you find anything—and I do mean *if*—you're not to announce your discoveries to anyone without my permission. That way, if the media does find out—"

"You'll know I was the one who leaked the news," Noelle finished for him.

Matt nodded. "I see we understand each other."

"Not quite," Noelle argued. "If I'm not allowed to notify the media, then I get to keep any fossils I find. That's right, keep," she replied to his unspoken question. "I can remove the fossils from your property without your expressed consent. They become my personal property. I'm talking full fossil ownership here."

"*Yours?* Not the museum's?"

"You got it." Noelle lifted her chin. "You said you only wanted to deal with me. If the museum owns the fossils, I can't vouch for their silence, now, can I? But if only *I* own them, I'll have no problem keeping a lid on things."

Noelle saw the surprise in his eyes for a bare instant. She'd seen that look before—it was the look of someone realizing she wasn't merely a pretty TV face.

"Let me get this straight," Matt said slowly. "If I give you the fossils, you keep them for yourself." Matt studied her closely. "Or sell them. Or chop them up into little pieces if you want."

"*Or* tempt another museum—a museum with international prestige—to hire me."

"Such as the Denver Museum of Natural History?"

"*Now* we understand each other," Noelle announced. "If the curators at the Denver museum want the fossils, they'll have to take me with them."

Matt's eyes narrowed. "A package deal, so to speak?"

"Exactly. I want future ownership of any fossils guaranteed, in writing. That's the price you'll pay for my work with the sponsors, plus my total silence during the two weeks I'm living at your ranch."

"Not acceptable. I want total silence until I say otherwise."

"For how long?"

"Until I say so. At the very most, until next summer. I don't care if you find a truckload of fossils and hold the world's largest bone auction. I don't want anyone, and I mean *anyone,* to know where they came from. I will *not* have my riders subjected to a three-ring circus. I need time to evaluate the situation."

"Hmm. I get the fossils, but I can't say where I found them until you give me permission?" Now it was Noelle's turn to cross her arms against her chest. "I *might* be able to live with that," she said slowly, "if you agree to one more condition."

"Don't push your luck, Dr. Forrest," Matt warned.

"Luck has nothing to do with this, Mr. Caldwell. I insist you hear me out. I have one more condition."

His voice was as hard as prehistoric granite. "And that is?"

"You let Jason Reilly in on this."

She saw her words take Matt totally by surprise. "Jason Reilly?"

"Yes. He'd make a great assistant for me. And since he already knows where the fossil came from, you should have no objection to his presence."

"You really want Jason to help you?" Matt asked incredulously.

"He's a great kid," Noelle said, immediately jumping to Jason's defense. "Smart as a whip, and full of enthusiasm. Any paleontologist would be glad to have him around. I want him to work with me."

An unreadable expression crossed Matt's face. "What if I say I like our deal the way it is now? Without Jason?"

"But—I told him I'd keep him posted! After all, he was the one who found the original fossil."

"Kids talk," Matt said, that same unfathomable look in his eyes. "They can't keep secrets. I don't want Jason blabbing to all his boys' club friends if you found more fossils."

"But he wouldn't, not if I explained it to him. He'd understand, I'm sure."

"Sorry. I said no help, and I *meant* no help."

Noelle stared at Matt. "But I promised!"

Matt shrugged. "He's just a kid. He'll get over it. So, yes or no? Do we have a deal or not?"

Suddenly Noelle understood how her sister Molly felt about her own children. Deeply protective and willing to sacrifice anything—the way she felt about Jason. It was a strange, unsettling, almost painful emotion, but Noelle's answer was never in doubt.

"No," she said quietly. "We don't."

"Sorry about that." Matt tossed her the car keys. "These negotiations are over."

She was so upset, she barely managed to catch her keys. "If you change your mind, you know where to reach me," she said with a trace of her old spirit. "And just for the record, I think you're a real sleaze where Jason is concerned. I'm glad you don't have any kids of your own. You don't deserve them."

She jammed the keys into the ignition, head held high. She then started to close the car door, but once again Matt held it open.

"Wait."

"Forget it! I'm leaving!" Noelle tugged at the inner door handle, trying to close it despite his grip on the outer handle.

"I've changed my mind."

"You *what?*"

"You heard me. Now that I've seen you have some actual consideration for children, I've changed my mind."

There was a moment of stunned silence on her part, then furious anger. "You deliberately tried to get me to break my promise to Jason!"

"Yes, I did," he admitted. "Consider this a little test of character, if you will. You get an A plus, Dinosaur Lady. It appears your affection for children isn't just a performance, after all."

Noelle's palm itched to slap that smug look off his face. It was only with the greatest control that she remained in her car. "Did you enjoy your little test, Mr. Caldwell? Did it give you a cheap thrill?"

"No. But Jason is a particular favorite of mine. And for *all* my patients' sakes, I had to see if you were the tough, hard-as-nails career woman you pretend to be."

"I *am* a tough, hard-as-nails career woman," Noelle flung back. "That doesn't mean I break promises to my friends, no matter how young they are."

"I can see that."

"Bully for you. Why don't you take out a front-page ad and tell the whole world while you're at it?"

"Not necessary. I only needed to see for myself."

There was reluctant, almost begrudging, admiration in his eyes. It wasn't a full-fledged endorsement, but Noelle didn't care. It was close enough. Matthew Caldwell was finally taking her seriously. She, on the other hand, had greatly underestimated *him*. She wouldn't make that mistake again.

Noelle studied him carefully. "You're hoping Jason's find was just a flash in the pan, aren't you? You don't want me finding *anything*."

"Let's just say a major find is the last thing those kids need."

"But you're going to let me try, anyway. Aren't you." It was a statement, not a question.

He nodded. "Two weeks, under the conditions we announced."

"Four."

He gave her a sharp glance.

"Four," she repeated. "Consider the extra time an apology for unfair negotiation practices."

"You're no pushover, Dinosaur Lady."

"And you play dirty, Mr. Ranch Owner."

Matt tilted his head and studied her.

"Three," he finally announced. "Three weeks, and that's my final offer. Take it or leave it."

He held out his hand for her to shake. "For the last time, Dr. Forrest—do we have a deal?"

Noelle thrust out her own hand. "Done," she said.

CHAPTER FOUR

"YOU GET TO STAY at Matt's for *three whole weeks?*" Jason asked for the umpteenth time as he watched Noelle pack.

The two were in Noelle's third-floor apartment. The Swansons were in the process of finalizing arrangements for another foster child, and Jason had begged to visit with Noelle instead of going along to the social worker's office. Noelle was more than willing, and after a few more phone conversations, Jason had been allowed to spend the afternoon with her.

"That's right. Three whole weeks." Noelle folded five pairs of brand-new, sturdy jeans and placed them in the suitcase. The jeans were for her field work—something she hadn't done much of since college.

"I wish I was going, too," Jason pouted. "We could look for fossils together—every single day." He sighed, a gusty, eleven-year-old's sigh of envy.

"I wish you could, too, Jason." She fondly ruffled his hair. "But remember what I told you. You're my assistant. If Mrs. Swanson says it's okay, you can stay late after your weekly riding lessons and help me out. And I'll drive you home."

"My next lesson's not until next week. I don't want to wait that long," Jason complained. He watched morosely as she added some durable cotton work shirts to the suitcase. "And I just know Mrs. Swanson won't want to take me to Matt's before then."

Noelle was positive Jason was right about that. Matt's ranch was over an hour's drive out of the city, and Mrs. Swanson's next foster child—a victim of physical abuse—

was presently in the hospital. With Jason and two daughters of her own, Mrs. Swanson had little enough free time as it was.

"Don't worry. I'll call you every evening," Noelle promised. "If I find anything—even the smallest fossil fragment—you'll hear about it."

"I still don't see why *I* can't stay at Matt's for three weeks," Jason said, still not mollified. "It's summer vacation. And Mrs. Swanson's so busy it's no fun at her house."

Noelle didn't like the way Jason said "at her house," as opposed to "at home." Gently she asked, "Aren't you happy where you live?"

Jason shrugged. "It's okay, I guess. The Swansons are nice."

"Don't the other children play with you?"

"They're not even in school yet. All they do is play baby games. Stuffed animals and dolls." Jason wrinkled his nose in distaste. "And I get stuck baby-sitting the girls when Mrs. Swanson has to go to the hospital."

"You baby-sit, Jason?"

"I *am* eleven," he said with injured dignity. "But it's pretty boring. Mrs. Swanson could always find someone else. Can't I come to Matt's with you?" he begged. "Please, Dinosaur Lady?"

Noelle stopped packing to give the boy a big hug. "Jason, if it were up to me, I'd take you in a minute. For the whole three weeks."

Jason lifted his head. "Really?" For a moment hope flooded his face.

"Really and truly. I know you'd make a great dig assistant." Noelle released him. "But it's not up to me, sweetheart. I'm not your legal guardian, and I'm just a guest in Matt's house. I can't take you along. I'm sorry."

Noelle expected a trembling chin or even tears. Instead, Jason was all smiles.

"If it's okay with *you,* then maybe it'll be okay with Mrs. Swanson. I know Matt won't mind," he said, his eyes sparkling with excitement. "I'm going to ask them, Dinosaur Lady."

"You're going to ask them?" Noelle echoed.

Jason gave a vigorous nod. "You *said* I'd make a great assistant. You *said* you wanted me along."

"Of course I do, but Jason . . . don't get your hopes up," she said uneasily. She hoped she wasn't setting the boy up for more disappointment. "I don't know if Mrs. Swanson will go along with this. Or Matt. Remember what we talked about? Matt wants this whole expedition kept secret."

"I know. But I'm going to ask anyway."

Noelle saw that Jason meant every word.

"Well, I'll keep my fingers crossed for you. But if things don't work out, please don't be too upset. Remember what I said. We'll get together after your weekly riding lesson. In between, I'll call you every night from Matt's. And I'll try to pop in and see you when I'm in town."

Jason had picked up a thick pair of work socks he was about to hand her. The socks froze in midair. "You'd leave your dig site to come and see *me?*" Jason asked.

Noelle had to laugh. "I have to *find* my dig site first, silly. And I'll be in town to tape my next *Fun with Fossils* show. So I'll definitely come visit. Even if I didn't have a taping, I'd still come."

"Really?"

"Really. Now pass me those socks. . . ."

CRIES OF "It's the Dinosaur Lady!" greeted Noelle as she stepped into Matt's office the next morning. Excited children—especially an overjoyed Jason Reilly—soon ensured a chaos of cries and questions.

"Jason, what are you doing here?" she asked. "I thought you'd already had your riding lesson this week." The chaos increased, and she had to raise her voice and repeat herself.

Noelle just barely managed to hear Jason's answer. He'd begged the Swansons to make a special trip out to the ranch to greet her. They were both there with their two daughters.

"I couldn't believe it when Jason told me his fossil was real," Mr. Swanson was saying. "I thought it was just his imagination. You know kids."

"I always knew Jason was a smart boy," Mrs. Swanson added. "He watches your show all the time."

"When are you going to find the rest of my dinosaur?" Jason asked eagerly, his voice drowning out both his foster parents and the other children in the room. "Can I come? Do I get to be on your show again?"

Noelle frantically looked around for the receptionist. She didn't want to disturb the office routine like she had on her last visit, but it appeared she was doing just that.

Only minutes later Matt emerged. As before, a few words from him reestablished order.

"Talk about déjà vu," she said ruefully. "I'm sorry about this. I tried to keep the noise down, but—"

"You're a celebrity." Matt took off his white medical coat to reveal jeans and a short-sleeved shirt beneath. He tossed the coat over a chair back, going from nurturing therapist to attractive male in one quick motion. "A certain amount of... bedlam is to be expected around celebrities."

Noelle felt her blood pressure rise at the thinly veiled censure. But because of the audience, she kept her cool.

"First of all, there's a big difference between bedlam and excitement," Noelle replied in an even tone. "And secondly, I'm a paleontologist. Educational television hardly qualifies me as the show-biz type. Take me out of the Denver area and very few people know who I am."

"You're too modest, Dr. Forrest. I understand your show's nationally syndicated."

"We've done well in the Four Corners area, California, and a couple of states back East," she admitted.

"More than a couple. I was told your show is seen in twenty-three states, total. That's almost half the nation."

"She's *famous*, Matt," Jason announced. "Everyone knows that."

"Well, I don't know about me, but you'll certainly be listed in the scientific records, Jason," Noelle assured him.

Jason swelled with pride.

"We're all very proud of you, Jason," Matt said kindly. "But right now I've got to get Dr. Forrest settled into her room."

"Can't we get her suitcase later?" Jason begged. "Let's show her the creek-bed trail."

"Jason, I don't think..." Matt broke off and looked around at the other children. "Wait a minute. You aren't my regular Saturday group. How many of you *aren't* here for regular appointments?"

At least five boys raised their hands. Noelle had already noticed that all of them were around Jason's age. But unlike Jason, none of them seemed to be candidates for Matt's special riding program. In fact, now that she thought about it, they all looked familiar.

"Who are you boys?"

Even before Jason answered, Noelle remembered. They'd been at the studio.

"They're from my boys' club," Jason piped up. "We all came to see Dr. Forrest."

Matt glared at Noelle. "Mr. Swanson, would you mind keeping an eye on these kids until my receptionist gets back from the stables? And Mrs. Swanson, if you and Dr. Forrest could step into my office for a moment..."

Noelle bit her lip. As soon as the door closed, she knew what was coming.

"I thought we agreed to keep this low-key, Dr. Forrest!"

"We did! And I explained it all to Jason."

"Then what's a whole damn boys' club doing here?" he demanded. "I told you I didn't need any publicity!"

"Matt, please." Mrs. Swanson laid a calming hand on Matt's arm. "I'm afraid this is my fault," she admitted. "I let Jason invite five of his special friends from the club. They came with us in our van. Jason was so excited, and since they were all at the studio when the fossil find was confirmed..."

"Did Jason explain to you why we want to keep this all quiet, Mrs. Swanson?" Noelle asked.

"Oh, yes. Jason hasn't told anyone else about the fossil. But the boys' club already knew."

Matt exhaled angrily. "Dammit, I forgot. Did anyone explain to *them* about keeping quiet? Dr. Forrest?"

Noelle shook her head.

"Mrs. Swanson?"

"Umm—I didn't, either" was Mrs. Swanson's nervous reply.

"Has Jason?"

"I—I don't know, Matt. But if they haven't, there's no harm done. I know they will. After all, they *are* Jason's friends. They can keep their word. I'll talk to them."

"Please do," Matt responded curtly. "If the boys have already talked to my patients, and they talk to their friends and parents, this could be the shortest-kept secret since gold was found at Sutter's Mill. I don't need the media competing with my patients for breathing space!"

"Matt, I'm so sorry. I should have checked with you first, but Jason was so excited . . ." Mrs. Swanson's face grew red with embarrassment. "Under the circumstances, maybe I should just take Jason and his friends home."

"No, they're already here. Let them stay," Matt decided. "Just go back in and try to do some damage control, please."

Mrs. Swanson ducked her head and quickly left.

"You needn't have been so hard on her!" Noelle immediately said as soon as they were alone. "You hurt her feelings!"

"Hurt feelings aren't a factor when it comes to the safety of my patients."

"But this wasn't her fault!" Noelle insisted.

"Damn right. The bulk of the blame belongs to you."

"Me?"

"Yes, you!" Matt stood stiffly before her, his arms crossed across his chest. "You haven't been here five minutes and you've caused trouble."

"I have not! You told me to be discreet, I *was* discreet! I didn't tell the boys' club about my fossil-hunting expedition!"

"You might as well have, because you didn't ask Mrs. Swanson not to say anything! You'll have the media out here before I know it. Maybe that omission was deliberate."

"It most certainly was not!" Noelle's cheeks flushed. "Has anyone ever told you that you've got a very suspicious mind?"

"You can't deny there's a lot at stake here. Perhaps you don't mind bending a few principles?"

"I'm sorry. I was excited, and it just slipped my mind."

Matt's lips thinned to a tight line. "That's no excuse. If you knew *anything* about children, you'd have thought to fill in the Swansons after talking to Jason."

"I know plenty about children, thanks," Noelle retorted. "And I know an eleven-year-old child doesn't need to be coddled. He's mature, responsible and sensible." Her expression plainly added, *Unlike you.* "Mrs. Swanson lets Jason baby-sit her daughters, crutches and all—so she trusts Jason Reilly's instincts. So do I. I refuse to treat him like a baby."

"You'll do whatever it takes to keep this ranch out of the news, Dr. Forrest, or you can get in your car and go back the way you came." Matt headed for the door. "Do I make myself clear?"

"Perfectly," she said in a stiff voice.

"Good. Let's go back outside."

The reception area was much quieter now. Noelle saw that many of the children were gone.

"The receptionist came back. She's walking the Saturday group down to the stables," Mr. Swanson informed Matt.

"And Matt, you'll be happy to hear Jason had already told his friends about the need for secrecy," Mrs. Swanson added with a relieved smile. "The boys've kept quiet about the fossil hunt. They didn't tell any of your patients."

Noelle shot Matt a triumphant look, but Jason forestalled any answer.

"Can't we get started, Dinosaur Lady?" Jason asked. "Can I get my horse now, Matt? I want to show Dr. Forrest and my friends where I found my fossil."

"We'll get your horse, Jason," Matt agreed. "But in the future, please clear it with me before you bring guests."

Jason nodded solemnly. "I will. Sorry, Matt." Then, in the same breath, "Are you ready, Dr. Forrest?"

"Just about," Noelle said, glad she'd worn jeans. "I have to run out to the car to get my knapsack and tools."

"Fine. While she's doing that, everyone who's here with Jason, follow me out to the stables," Matt ordered.

A few minutes later Noelle rejoined them.

"I'm sorry about all this," Noelle said in an undertone to Mrs. Swanson once they were outside. "I didn't mean to cause you or Jason any problems."

"It's okay," Mrs. Swanson said. "I really should have called. And Jason can be quite determined when he sets his mind on something."

"So can Matt," Noelle grumbled. The man had no patience—at least with her. She couldn't understand how anyone working with children day in and day out could have such a short fuse.

"I need to saddle up a horse for Jason," Matt said outside the stable entrance. "The rest of you who want to come along will have to hike the trail. Mr. and Mrs. Swanson, if you'd please keep an eye on everyone else, I'll tend to Jason."

"Come on, Dr. Forrest," Jason urged as Noelle remained with the group of children. "Matt didn't mean for *you* to wait outside."

Noelle was just as certain Matt *had* meant that, but she followed Jason and Matt into the stables, anyway. Matt retrieved the special harness Jason had to use, then saddled a horse for Jason and one for himself.

"What about you, Dr. Forrest?" Jason asked curiously. "Aren't you riding?"

"I'm afraid I, uh, don't know how," Noelle replied. "I'll walk with the rest of your friends."

"You could ride with me," Matt suggested, raising one eyebrow.

"No, thanks." Noelle flattened herself against a stall door as Matt led the two horses outside and tied them to the hitching post. She wondered if it was the horses or the man himself that made her feel so anxious. The thought of the two of them on horseback, her arms wrapped tightly around his waist, certainly had her nerves crackling with excess energy....

"Don't you like horses?" Jason asked.

"I think they're beautiful animals. But I can look for fossils better on my feet than from high above the ground."

"It's a long walk," Matt warned as he returned for her and Jason.

"It can't be that bad if you're letting the other children come along," Noelle retorted. "Don't worry about me. I'll keep up."

She watched Matt shrug, then turn his attention to Jason. "Ready, son?"

Jason nodded. He handed Noelle his crutches and let Matt lift him into the saddle. The horse, a small pony, was docile as Jason strapped his legs into the specially adapted tack.

Matt watched carefully, then nodded with approval. "All right, Jason. You and I will lead the way."

Noelle rejoined the rest of the children and Jason's foster parents, and the expedition was off. Mr. Swanson carried Jason's crutches while Mrs. Swanson minded her two girls. The five boys were torn between talking to the "Dinosaur Lady" and watching their friend atop a horse. That situation soon changed when Matt offered to give each of Jason's friends a turn riding his own horse.

Noelle watched Matt instantly become a hero to five young boys. Mr. Swanson helped the boys off and on while Matt kept the horse calm. Then Matt would slowly lead the horse, the men walking on either side to make sure the novice riders didn't fall off.

Despite the tedium of stopping for each boy to mount and dismount, Matt continued to give long, leisurely rides to everyone who wanted them. She noticed how comfortable the boys were around Matt. It was amazing how a man who had such rapport with children could be so prickly around her. It was even more amazing how much that bothered her.

Noelle's popularity had waned as Matt became the center of attention. But she didn't mind. She enjoyed seeing the boys' pleasure just as much as Matt seemed to. And without the children clamoring around her, she was able to talk freely to Mrs. Swanson. After a few pleasantries, she ventured to ask when it would be convenient for Jason to appear on her next *Fun with Fossils* episode.

"Whenever you want," Mrs. Swanson answered with a smile. "Jason's so crazy about you and your show that the sooner the better is probably best. He'll go berserk, otherwise."

"I'm sorry if Jason's dino-mania has gone overboard. Ever since that movie, every kid in town is dinosaur crazy, not just Jason."

"*Jurassic Park?*"

"Yes. It may have been a smash hit, but it wasn't exactly an accurate representation of my profession," Noelle said wryly.

"Oh, but the movie had nothing to do with Jason's enthusiasm for fossils," Mrs. Swanson hastened to say. "It had everything to do with you."

"Me?" Noelle was flabbergasted.

The other woman nodded. "Let me start from the beginning. Jason wasn't always on crutches, you know...."

She abruptly stopped talking and shooed her two daughters on ahead, then continued the story when they were out of earshot.

"According to Jason's caseworker, he was a very active baby who grew into a very active young boy. His father was—is—in prison, and his teenage mother couldn't handle him. Jason was always full of adventure." She sighed. "He fell from a tree a little over two years ago. The spinal damage required hospitalization. His mother abandoned him when she heard the damage was permanent. He'll be in leg braces and crutches the rest of his life."

"Oh, no!"

"Yes, I'm afraid so. Jason was made a ward of the courts, and then he came into our hands. For a while we were extremely concerned about his emotional state. Between his mother's defection and his injuries, he was in bad shape.

"Jason wouldn't talk," she went on. "He wouldn't co-operate with his therapist. He wouldn't even eat. We thought he'd never be able to leave the hospital. Jason would lie and stare at the television for hours, totally shutting himself off from the outside world. Then one day he saw your show."

Mrs. Swanson sighed. "We'd been praying for a miracle, and *Fun with Fossils* was it, Dr. Forrest. Jason started watching it in the hospital.

"It was the first thing he showed any interest in after his accident. He told us he wanted to get better so he could hunt for fossils."

"How amazing!" Noelle could barely speak. Awe mixed with pleasure. Her little show had actually touched some-one's life for the better.

Mrs. Swanson smiled. "Jason swore some day he'd come on your show and give you a dinosaur bone himself."

Noelle blinked with amazement and stopped walking. "And he actually did! What a remarkable coincidence!"

Mrs. Swanson shook her head. "No, Dr. Forrest. It was no coincidence. Jason was determined to learn all he could about fossils. He demanded a wheelchair so he could get to the library and read about dinosaurs. He started eating, doing his exercises and learning to get around on crutches.

"It was incredible. It was like having a totally different child. Jason asked for tapes of *Fun with Fossils*. He watched all your shows over and over again. He even took notes on them."

Her husband approached then and joined the conversation. "Jason couldn't wait to go back to school so he could learn more. He also wanted to learn to ride a horse so he could cover more ground while looking for fossils."

"And he did," Mrs. Swanson said proudly. "Jason's been hunting for dinosaur bones both on and off a horse since he was released from the hospital last summer. Even the boys' club field trip to your studio was his idea."

"I know you don't need us all tagging along," Mr. Swanson said quietly, "and we didn't mean to upset Matt.

But I hope you can understand why we were reluctant to keep Jason and his friends home today.''

Mrs. Swanson touched Noelle's shoulder gratefully. ''You've been his inspiration, Dr. Forrest. Without you and Mr. Caldwell, who knows what might have happened to Jason.''

There was silence. Noelle's throat was tight as she watched Jason happily talking to the boys walking beside his horse. ''Thank you for telling me,'' she finally said. ''I'm glad I was able to help.''

''We're both so happy for Jason. He's doing so well that we're hoping the social worker will soon decide he's eligible for adoption.''

''*Adoption?*'' Noelle's pleasure suddenly faded, to be replaced by a strange pain deep inside. ''But aren't you...?'' Her voiced trailed off.

''No, we're not,'' Mr. Swanson said firmly. ''In addition to caring for Jason and the children who have preceded him, we have a son away at college and two daughters of our own. All three were originally foster children we adopted, I might add.''

Mrs. Swanson's smile held a trace of sadness. ''Dr. Forrest, we can't possibly adopt all the foster children who come into our lives. We have to settle for loving them for a short time and preparing them for a permanent home. I know it must sound coldhearted....''

''Oh, no,'' Noelle replied quickly. ''I'm just glad Jason has people like you to look out for him.''

''And people like you, Dr. Forrest. And Matt,'' Mr. Swanson said. Noelle murmured her thanks; then the Swansons hurried to catch up with their daughters.

Noelle remained rooted to the spot, thinking about what the Swansons had told her. She watched Jason's laughing face and wondered who his next parents would be. Or would he remain a ward of the courts until he was eighteen? *Probably the latter,* she thought sadly. Noelle knew most people wanted to adopt healthy babies, not older, handicapped children. Poor Jason. Even though he was obviously well cared for, it wasn't the same as having a permanent home or real parents.

Too bad I don't have a stable career, Noelle thought. Or was at least married to someone who did. She just might be tempted to take Jason in herself. But she wasn't married, and it was foolish to pretend she'd have any chance as a single parent. Her professional future was iffy at best, and a boy like Jason—a boy whose biological father was in prison—needed a strong male role model in his life. She'd never make it past the first interview with a social worker.

Which was a shame, really. Jason was a great kid. Noelle hoped someday Jason would get the family every child deserved to have.

She stood silent for so long that Matt stopped his horse and called back to her. "Are you all right, Dr. Forrest?"

"I'm fine," she said. "I was just taking a breather."

She started walking along the trail again, but some of the joy had gone out of the expedition. After the Swansons' revelations about Jason's background, everything else—even reaching the original fossil site—seemed almost anticlimactic. But the children's enthusiasm was catching, and soon she'd recaptured her earlier spirit. As Mr. Swanson helped Jason dismount, Noelle roused herself enough to attend to the job at hand.

She was used to most adults believing that paleontology was a dull business at best. Not so with children. The primary method of operation was digging in the dirt, and the boys were only too happy to assist.

"Are you sure this is where you found the fossil, Jason?"

Noelle opened her knapsack and passed out one of her three trowels to an eager helper. The other children would have to dig with their hands.

"I'm sure." Jason inspected the area, then accepted the second trowel as the others waited for instructions. "See that old dead tree? I remembered it for my landmark, just like you said on your show."

"You're quite the expert, Jason," Matt said from behind her. Noelle turned to find Matt approaching them with long, easy strides. He'd tied the two horses up on the bank, away from the gravel-bottomed creek bed. "What do we do next?"

She lifted up her own trowel. "We dig, of course. If there's anything to be found, it makes sense to look in the vicinity of the original find. With loose gravel beds like these, sometimes we can spot something within the first two to three feet of soil."

Jason looked to Noelle eagerly, an eagerness that faded somewhat as Matt said, "We can't have gaping holes here in the trail. The horses could stumble and injure a rider."

"We'll fill everything back in," Noelle assured him. "I should be able to make some assumptions about this area without digging very deep."

Jason immediately clamored for Mr. Swanson to pass him his crutches. Noelle positioned first Jason, then the other children, then everyone started digging. Matt simply watched.

"Aren't you going to dig, too, Matt?" Jason asked.

"Not yet, son. I have to leave in a few minutes to get back to a patient. I thought I'd just watch." He turned his attention to Noelle. "What's Jason supposed to be looking for?"

"Well, sometimes you'll find bare bones. But that's rare. More often they'll be partially or completely encased in rock. I try to look for something different from the medium in which I'm digging."

"So if the boys see something that doesn't look like the usual gravel bottom, they yell?"

"Yes. Large porous rocks in gravel would be suspicious. A color other than this gray-brown would be suspicious." She stabbed at the ground with her trowel. "And of course anything resembling bony material is a red flag."

"Wouldn't it be easier to dig with a shovel?"

"Sometimes. But you can't dig as if you're digging fencepost holes," she warned. "With loose soil like this, you have to take small, gentle shovelfuls. If we find bone that's not encased in rock or isn't permineralized—"

"Which means?" Matt asked.

"The bone cavities have been filled and solidified with minerals."

"Like being petrified," Jason threw in.

"Exactly. Jason, didn't you ever show Matt your original fossil?" Noelle asked.

"Nope."

"Why not?"

"I wanted *you* to see it," Jason said, and went back to digging.

"I'm afraid you jumped the gun there, Jason," Noelle said ruefully.

"I agree. Jason, I don't mind that you found the fossil, but you shouldn't just have taken it," Matt said in a calm voice. "Next time, you come tell me, okay?"

Noelle was impressed by the way Matt got his point across without embarrassing the boy.

"That's right, Jason. Other landowners might not be as understanding as Mr. Caldwell."

"I thought it was 'finders, keepers, losers, weepers.'"

"That does *not* apply here," Noelle said firmly.

"It certainly doesn't." Matt turned toward her, his expression clearly disapproving. "Perhaps you should do a *Fun with Fossils* show on the legalities of fossil ownership, Dr. Forrest. It might save you a lot of trouble in the future."

"I don't need—" She'd started to tell him she didn't need anyone to tell her how to do her job, but Jason's wide eyes stopped her. She bit back the angry words.

"I'll take the matter under advisement," Noelle said instead with a brittle smile. Then she deftly changed the subject. "We've gotten away from the original question, Mr. Caldwell. You were asking why I didn't use a shovel."

She gestured toward the ground with a hand that was much steadier than the feeling inside her stomach.

"If the fossil *hasn't* been permineralized, the bone will be fragile, and strong shovel strokes will break it. That's why we use trowels. Sometimes even they can do damage. Speaking of which, I should go check on the other children. Please excuse me."

She walked away, reflecting on the irony of a fancy education that had never helped her locate a fossil, while a child who knew absolutely nothing about ownership legalities had blithely carried one home.

Still, she managed to hide her feelings. As much as she hated to admit it, Matt was right. She probably should touch on ownership legalities—should have done so when Jason presented her with the fossil. But she'd been so excited, and Jason had been so proud. Even if she'd had the presence of mind to question him, she wouldn't have wanted to spoil the boy's pleasure.

Too bad Matt Caldwell didn't feel the same way about her *pleasure.* Her first day out on a dig since grad school, and it was ruined already.

But none of that showed on her face. Noelle went from child to child, making certain everyone followed the correct procedures and felt a part of the dig. She'd just finished talking to the last boy when Matt approached. She tried to avoid him, but he caught up to her just the same.

"Jason seems to think I've hurt your feelings, Dr. Forrest," he said quietly. "Have I?"

"Don't be ridiculous," she scoffed.

There was no way in this world she'd let him know the truth. He *had* hurt her feelings, deeply so. Matt seemed to treat her as either a superficial TV personality or a hard-bitten, ambitious woman who wasn't above lying or manipulation to get what she wanted. And either way, he was making his lack of respect for her plainly apparent. That hurt.

"I wasn't trying to tell you how to do your job." His words sounded sincere, even apologetic.

"Of course you were," she wearily replied. "But I can't complain. Between your original accusations as to my blackmailing, child-hating character, and then what you said today, back in your office... Telling me how to do my job is a step up."

Matt flinched. For a second she wondered if she'd finally rendered him speechless, then decided she was wrong as his habitual air of control resurfaced. He opened his mouth, but she cut him off with a wave of her hand.

"I know what you're going to say. And please, I've heard it before. You're only trying to protect your patients, right? If you want a blanket excuse for your behavior, I imagine that's as good as any. But you'll have to forgive me if I'm tired of listening to it."

She turned to head back to Jason's location, but a firm hand on her arm stopped her.

"*Now* what?"

"I *did* hurt your feelings. Dr. Forrest, I'm sorry."

"You didn't, so don't worry about it. Please let go. Jason's waiting." She tried to pull away, but although the grip on her arm wasn't painful, it was strong. She wasn't going anywhere.

"Wait a minute. While we were riding down here, Jason asked if he could spend three weeks on the ranch with us."

Noelle grew still, and Matt pressed on.

"He said you'd love to have him work with you."

"Yes, that's true. But I didn't encourage him, if that's what you're suggesting," she said defensively. "I told him you and the Swansons probably wouldn't allow it."

"Jason told me that, too. At first, I didn't think the whole thing was a good idea. But Jason seems to be pretty good at this paleontology stuff. Look at him."

They both watched Jason busily demonstrating procedures, and in general taking charge. Even his foster parents gave themselves up to Jason's confident air and knowledge.

"He certainly knows what he's talking about," Matt remarked. "And I know Jason lives, breathes and eats dinosaurs. He's a different kid when he's with you."

Noelle's arm was finally released, but she remained in place. "Just what are you trying to say?"

"Jason's a particular favorite of mine. He's not exactly the happiest child around, but he positively glows when he's with you. I think letting Jason stay with us is a good idea."

Noelle could barely contain her excitement. "You really wouldn't mind?"

"Not at all," Matt assured her. "Mrs. Swanson is extremely busy right now. She's spending a lot of time at the hospital trying to build a relationship with her next foster child. Mr. Swanson works, so his wife has her hands full with Jason and the girls."

"Go on," Noelle said.

"Jason wants to stay with us, Mrs. Swanson could use a break, and you did say you needed an assistant. I'm sure the Swansons would let Jason stay at the ranch." He studied her carefully. "If you still want him, that is."

"Of course I do!" Noelle's eyes narrowed. "But I'm curious. Why have you suddenly changed your mind?"

"Number one, you let Jason appear on your show—in front of the cameras and thousands of viewers. Many people are uncomfortable around the handicapped, but you didn't try to sweep the boy under the carpet."

"Why should I? Jason's a perfectly delightful child!"

"Not everyone would do what you did. Number two," Matt went on, "Jason's had enough unhappiness in his life. He deserves a break. And number three..." Matt looked at her with an odd expression in his eyes. "Well, let's just say I've decided you deserve a break, too."

Noelle blinked. "Let me get this straight. You're actually going to let Jason be my full-time assistant?"

"If his foster parents agree, yes. And I'm sure they will."

"You're actually declaring a truce?" She couldn't believe her ears.

"Why not? We're both interested in Jason's welfare. I'm sure we can be civil to each other. We can even start using first names—unless you prefer being called the Dinosaur Lady."

Noelle was completely taken by surprise at his words—and the attractive smile that accompanied them. She stared at him for a few seconds until astonishment was replaced by a thrill of pleasure. And then her defenses rose again.

"No, I prefer Noelle," she said cautiously. *At least, until I hit pay dirt. Then you can call me Dr. Forrest.*

CHAPTER FIVE

"DO YOU THINK WE'LL FIND any fossils today, Dinosaur Lady?" Jason asked hopefully.

Noelle, Matt and Jason were gathered for breakfast in the large, cheerful kitchen of the sprawling ranch house. Noelle had been at the ranch for a week now, and Jason never failed to ask her the same question at every meal. She didn't disappoint him.

"I'm keeping my fingers crossed, Jason. Today could be the day."

Jason crossed his own fingers and held them up for her to see. "I hope so." He'd finished breakfast, grabbed his crutches and cleared his dirty dishes from the table. "I'll go make my bed, then I'll be ready to go, Dinosaur Lady."

"I'll be waiting," Noelle replied with a smile. She watched as Jason hobbled out of the kitchen to his first-floor bedroom.

"Looks like we might be in for some rain today. Are you still going fossil hunting?" Matt asked.

To Noelle's secret delight, his question held concern, not censure. Ever since they'd declared a truce, they'd gotten along fairly well. As for the few uncomfortable moments, Jason was always there as a buffer. His enthusiastic presence certainly inhibited negative emotions.

"Clouds are really building," Matt continued. "I've already had several calls canceling afternoon lessons."

"It's not that cloudy yet," Noelle replied. "If it does start raining, I'll immediately walk Jason back. Unless you don't want me to take him today."

Matt looked out the huge kitchen window. "I'd hate to see him get soaked. Or you."

"We'll be fine," Noelle replied, oddly pleased that he'd included her in his concern. "We both know enough to come in out of the rain."

"Well, you be careful," Matt warned. "Oh, I probably won't see you and Jason at lunchtime," he added. "I'll be at the airport picking up Alex." With that, Matt left the room. Noelle remembered what Jason had told her—that Alex Caldwell had left town on an extended horse-buying trip. She had yet to meet Matt's brother. Perhaps she'd finally see him at dinner. Funny, Matt never talked about Alex. But then, Matt wasn't one to talk about his personal life. He was too busy with his patients or doing paperwork for his lobby group.

Work was okay in itself, Noelle thought as she carried her cup and cereal bowl to the dishwasher. But she'd thought that Matt would have opened up to her a little more by now. Instead, he talked to Jason, or she talked to Jason, or Jason talked to them both. There was very little direct communication between the two adults. To Noelle's dismay, they never seemed to find much common ground aside from their affection for Jason.

It wasn't as if she was some shy wallflower, for goodness' sake! She was an intelligent woman who could hold her own in any conversation. She wasn't a slob, either; she always bathed and changed her dirty work clothes for dinner, and made certain Jason did the same. Yet no matter how sparkling her personality or how attractive her appearance, Matt invariably ended up at his desk doing ranch paperwork while she sat on the sofa doing her own work. Watching Matt's back and bent head hardly made for the most sociable evenings.

When Jason went to clean up and change for bed, a task with which he needed no help whatsoever, Matt generally disappeared to check on the horses one last time. Noelle would watch him leave. As he often went for a moonlight ride afterward, he rarely came back to the house until long after Noelle had retired for the night.

In the meantime, she usually ended up compiling her notes on the day's dig and making follow-up calls to potential sponsors. She was determined to keep her end of the bargain. And after it was too late for phone calls, she'd curl up with a book or watch a sit-com on television in a vain attempt to cheer herself up.

Strange how Matt's lack of attention added to the disappointment of her so-far fruitless fossil search. It wasn't that she'd expected much from Matt, but she'd at least thought they'd be able to socialize. She missed adult company and found herself craving his. Even phone conversations with Molly left her curiously lonely.

Seeing him work with patients had shown her a very appealing side of Matt Caldwell. She knew he had a temper and could be fierce when it came to his patients' welfare. But he also had a ready smile, a kind word and a gentle touch for anyone who needed him. Except, perhaps, her...

Noelle had remembered Jason's words about Matt and the female therapist, Connie. She'd surreptitiously watched the two during the times she'd seen them together, and saw that Matt was indeed just friendly with the other woman. Connie, both intelligent and attractive, seemed nice enough. It made Noelle curious. Just what kind of women would Matt *really* be interested in? Would it have hurt him to talk to her once in a while? The fact that he hadn't stung more than she would admit.

Well, at least she had a fan in Jason, she consoled herself. Jason was ecstatically happy in his role as her assistant. And maybe the conversation would liven up when Alex came home.

Noelle had studied Alex Caldwell in the family picture on the mantel. Matt's younger brother was lightly built and delicately colored. He didn't present the firm aura of strength and self-assurance that both Matt and his father had. But then, the picture must have been taken a decade ago. It would be interesting to see Matt's younger brother in person. Maybe Alex would be the one to break the ice.

Because if it wasn't for mealtimes, Noelle doubted she'd see Matt at all....

"Are you ready to go, Jason?" she called down the hall. "I am if you are."

"Here I come," Jason sang out. He hurried to her with such a wide grin that Noelle's spirits couldn't help lifting.

"Then let's go outside and get started."

She and Jason had worked out their routine. They rose early to have breakfast with Matt. Noelle would ready her tools while Jason did his chores. Then, after getting mounted and tying his crutches to the specially adapted tack, Jason rode while she hiked out to the creek bed. From there, they spent the day digging at likely looking off-trail locations around the original site.

So far they'd come home for lunch every day. The walk made a good break, and there'd been nothing for Noelle to tear herself away from. Of course, coming back empty-handed for lunch was nowhere near as disappointing as coming back in the late afternoon with nothing to show for yet another day of hard work.

"Is everything okay, Dr. Forrest?" Jason asked as this particular afternoon went on and her luck went nowhere. They were both digging, Jason busy with his trowel, while Noelle cleared away some brush with a small folding shovel.

"I'm getting tired of finding only weeds," Noelle complained with a particularly vicious *whack* at a thorny cluster.

"You said on your show that paleontologists need to be patient people," Jason responded primly.

"I know. But knowing and doing are two different things. This is *not* what I went to grad school for!"

She wiped her sweaty forehead with a soiled shirtsleeve. Then, in a fit of temper, she tossed her shovel to the ground.

"Hey, careful there! You almost got my horse!"

"Hi, Matt!" Jason shouted.

Noelle looked up to see Matt on horseback, his lips curved in amusement. "This is an aspect of dinosaur hunting I've never seen before."

Her own good humor suddenly returned. He'd never ridden out to see them before. And frankly, considering how the day was going, she welcomed the distraction.

"Don't be so surprised," she said, breaking out into a rueful smile. "I do lose my cool now and then."

Matt dismounted and tied his horse to a nearby tree. "I can see why." He came closer to peer into one of the roped-off grids where she'd been digging. "It looks like hot, dirty work to me."

"It is, especially when you don't find anything. What I really need is some of Jason's luck. Right, Jason?"

Jason nodded and preened a bit. Noelle peeled off her leather gloves and tossed them after the shovel.

"Well, cheer up. You still have two more weeks to go." Matt spotted the canteens. He uncapped hers and Jason's, and passed them over.

"Thanks." She took a heavenly swig, washing away the bitter taste of dirt and disappointment. "Speaking of work, what are you doing out here? You said you had to go to the airport to pick up your brother."

"Alex took an earlier flight and grabbed a cab. I'm done for the day, and I thought you might want to come in a little early to meet him."

"No!" Jason suddenly argued. "We're not ready to leave yet!"

"Jason!" Noelle was frankly shocked. It was the first time she'd seen Jason so rude. Unless they were out fossil hunting, Jason usually adored being with Matt.

"Tell him we're busy, Dinosaur Lady," Jason insisted.

"But Jason, I've never met Alex. I should at least say hello to him. Don't you want to come with me?"

Jason remained defiantly silent and continued to dig with his trowel.

"Please pack up your things, Jason," Matt said firmly. "You know I don't allow riders out alone."

An angry Jason reached for his crutches and made his way to the pony he always rode.

"I've never seen Jason so upset. What was that all about?" Noelle asked when Jason was out of earshot.

"It's not hard to explain. I don't think Jason wants to share you with anyone."

"*What?*"

"Jason's jealous. Don't tell me it's escaped your notice." He gave Jason a sideways glance to make sure the boy wasn't listening. "He has a king-size crush on you."

"Don't be ridiculous! It's my *job* Jason's crazy about."

Matt shook his head. "It's more than that. In fact, now that I think about it, he's at the right age, too."

"Oh, Matt, really! You see romance from a man's point of view, not a boy's. I don't think you're in any position to judge Jason's feelings toward me."

"And you are?"

"Yes. I deal with little fans like Jason all the time."

Both watched Jason from a distance. As the angry boy paid no attention to the adults' conversation, Matt ventured to say, "I've know Jason much longer than you have, Dr. Forrest. And unlike you, I was a boy once myself. I remember my first crush on one of my teachers. It was very real to me, and I wasn't much older than Jason. So I'm warning you—don't encourage him. After two more weeks you go back to your bright lights and glamorous job, while he goes back to his foster home. He has enough to handle without a case of infatuation, too."

"There's no infatuation involved here," Noelle insisted. "It's more like..." She paused.

What *was* it, anyway? Noelle picked up the folding shovel and collapsed it, collecting her thoughts. Whatever relationship she shared with Jason had nothing to do with boyish crushes or a fan's adoration. What they shared felt much more intense. It was almost like...like what? she wondered, still confused. *Mother and child, perhaps?*

"We're friends," she finally stated. "Nowhere is it written that a child can't have adult friends."

"Are you two coming or not?" a sullen voice called out.

Both Matt and Noelle looked up. "We're coming, Jason."

"This subject isn't closed," Matt said in an undertone.

Noelle's response was to gather up the rest of her tools and put on her knapsack. Matt helped Jason mount, then mounted up himself. As the riders reined onto the trail,

Noelle joined them, keeping a safe distance from the horses, but still within talking distance.

"So, Jason, what's it like working with the Dinosaur Lady?" Matt asked.

Jason merely shrugged. Matt frowned, and Noelle hurried to fill the gap.

"Well, we may not have found anything yet, but it's great working outside." Noelle gestured toward the rolling expanse of land before them. "This is a welcome change for me."

"It would be better if we made a find," Jason mumbled.

"Well, that goes without saying," Noelle said with forced cheerfulness. "But right now my back's aching and—"

"Don't tell me you've been a celebrity too long to enjoy fieldwork?"

Noelle blinked. "Heavens, Matt, I've told you before—I'm no celebrity. I'm a long way off from limousines and bodyguards. And I certainly don't mind getting my hands dirty." She thought for a moment. "I'd love to be a paleontologist full-time. But what I'd miss is seeing youngsters like Jason, watching their eyes grow wide when I tell them something new. I'd miss their reactions when I show them how exciting paleontology can be. I guess I'd miss..." She spread her hands wide as she groped for the words.

"Someone to share it with?"

"Yes," Noelle said, impressed by his insight. She hadn't even realized it herself until just now. "I suppose I would. That's what makes having Jason along with me so special." She gave the boy a brilliant smile. "I'd be awfully lonely without my favorite assistant." Noelle was rewarded as Jason visibly thawed.

"Well, if you ever make the find of the century, you'll have an audience beyond your wildest expectations," Matt said. "Your name in the newspapers and on television. Your photograph on the cover of *National Geographic*. The works."

"I want to be on the cover, too!" Jason added.

"You, too, Jason? Is that what you really want? A lot of foolish publicity over a bunch of dead bones?"

Noelle considered such a future. "I have to admit it would be nice...."

"Nice?" Jason exploded. "It would be *fantastic!*"

"Yes. But somehow I don't think it would compete with the pleasure I get from teaching people like you, Jason. Fossils or no fossils, when these three weeks are up, the worst part will be having to say goodbye to you."

She took in Jason's amazed face, and was amazed herself to see a sudden telltale brightness in his eyes. Then he spurred his horse to a quick trot and hurried ahead. Noelle guessed he didn't want to embarrass himself. Her nephew hated for anyone to see him cry. She turned to Matt for reassurance.

Reassurance was not what she saw in his eyes. What she saw was anger.

"What did we just finish talking about? I thought I told you not to encourage him!" Matt hissed.

"I wasn't! I just said what was in my head."

"Then I suggest you think first and speak afterward!"

"It wouldn't hurt for you to do the same," she retorted.

"Me?" Matt glared down at her from atop his horse.

"Yes, you! All you've done is complain about my presence and moan about what havoc I'll create if I find any fossils."

"That's the truth."

"So what if it is? The question's strictly academic. Jason's find—as marvelous as it was—might be the only one on your land. The odds of finding even partial fossil pieces are astronomical."

"Your point, Dr. Forrest?"

"The point is, since this is probably a wild-goose chase, anyway, it wouldn't hurt you to show a little more enthusiasm when you're around Jason," she flung back at him. "The kid doesn't need you deliberately crushing his hopes."

There was a stunned silence from Matt.

"That's right," Noelle said, driving her point home. "If you really care for Jason, if you have any sensitivity at all, let him talk about fossils. Let him make believe he's the next Jim Jensen on the cover of *National Geographic*. Let him wish for a whole damn skeleton if he wants. So what if he has a better chance winning the lottery? It won't kill you to pretend! It won't even cost you anything. Let Jason have his dream!''

She exhaled angrily.

"You know, I thought better of you, Matt Caldwell. But it appears I made a mistake." She dared to look up at him again as she continued her hike beside his horse.

Matt met her gaze, then his eyes were on Jason ahead of them. Finally he turned back toward her.

"You're right."

Noelle nearly stumbled in shock. "You're actually admitting you were wrong?"

"Don't look so surprised," he replied tersely. "I'm not infallible, nor am I stubborn. I intend to make sure I don't belittle his hopes again. And *you* should discourage his crush on you."

"And I'm telling you, he doesn't have a crush on me!" Noelle insisted. "What's more, I can prove it."

"How?"

"Have Jason wait for us, and I'll ask you to give me a ride on your horse. If Jason acts jealous, then I'll concede your point. If he doesn't mind me cozying up to you, then you'll admit you're wrong about this, too. And drop it."

"Fair enough." Matt studied her. "But I thought you were afraid of horses."

"I said I was *nervous* around horses. Besides, I'm not actually going to get on one. I'll merely *ask* you for a ride and see how Jason responds. That should do the trick." She gestured in the boy's direction and said, "Ride on ahead and have Jason wait for me to catch up. I'll take it from there."

Matt shook his head but did as she asked. Noelle picked up her pace. When she had caught up to the horses and had Jason's attention, Noelle pointedly checked her watch.

"We're all going to be late for lunch at this rate. Alex must be waiting for us. Matt, do you mind giving me a ride?"

"You're certain?"

Her answer was to hand Matt her backpack to tie onto his saddlebags. "Jason, you don't mind if Matt gives me a ride, do you?"

There it was, another one of Jason's irritating shrugs for an answer. *If I was his mother, that's one habit I'd break right away,* she found herself thinking. She also realized that Jason's face told her nothing. She'd have to keep up the act a bit longer.

Noelle stared at Matt's extended hand, and then at the horse. Suddenly Matt's horse seemed even larger than before. And those steel-shod feet.... She really hadn't planned to get this close to a horse, let alone actually get on.

"Change your mind?" Matt asked with feigned innocence.

She scowled at him. "Of course not. I was, uh, just wondering how one rides."

"I'll do the riding. You just sit and hold on."

"Sounds good to me." *Yeah, right. And CMP is going to offer me a tenured position tomorrow.*

"Are you scared?" Jason asked.

"Umm, maybe just a bit."

"You'll like it, Dinosaur Lady," he said confidently. "Matt's a good rider. He taught me, and I was scared at first, too."

Well, that was a good sign, Noelle decided. Jason didn't seem to be jealous of Matt at all. She hoped she'd proved her point. Maybe she could back out of this horse thing right now.

"You really should learn to ride, Dinosaur Lady. You can scout for dig sites a lot easier on horseback than on foot," Jason added.

Never in a million years, she told herself. *That's why they built Jeeps. Jeeps don't bite or kick.*

"Matt could teach you, and I could help you learn about horses. I'm not as good a teacher as you, but I could try."

Noelle paused, her fear temporarily pushed into the background. Somehow Jason's words made her job at *Fun with Fossils* seem more important, made her little show seem more valuable.

"That means a lot to me, Jason," she said with a catch in her throat. "Thank you."

"You're welcome, Dinosaur Lady." He grinned. "I can't wait to see you on horseback."

Oh, damn and double damn. Why did Jason have to look at her with worship in his eyes? No way in the world could she back away from this now.

"I'm looking forward to it, Jason," she lied.

"But I thought . . ." Matt started to protest.

Noelle gave him a fierce look that plainly said, "Keep quiet!" Matt did.

"Okay, guys, how do I get on?" she asked.

"First you take a deep breath and try to relax," Matt replied.

Noelle puffed out a quick inhalation. "I'm relaxed."

Matt raised one eyebrow skeptically. "Take in a few more breaths. That's better. Now, climb up on that boulder over there. We'll use it for a mounting post."

Noelle did as she was directed, and swallowed hard. "He won't kick me, will he?"

"He won't kick you," Jason told her. "All Matt's horses are good and gentle."

"That's right," Matt assured her. "Now I'll come closer, but you just stand there. Don't do anything until I tell you."

"Don't worry, I won't." Noelle watched nervously as Matt lined his horse up with her rock.

"First, place your hands on my shoulders."

As she did so, Matt whispered, "You don't have to go through with this, Noelle. I know you're scared. And so does the horse."

"I told you I'd prove Jason doesn't have a crush on me," she whispered back. "I said I'd do this, and I will."

"Everything all right, Dinosaur Lady?" Jason asked as he observed the inaudible exchange.

"Just fine," she answered through gritted teeth.

"I'm going to take my right foot out of the stirrup," Matt said. "When you're ready, put *your* right foot in, then swing your left leg over the horse. Sit yourself directly behind my saddle and put your arms around my waist. Got that?"

Noelle nodded. "He won't run away, will he?"

"He'll stand quietly," Jason said at the same time Matt said, "No, he's well schooled."

The two males grinned. Noelle noticed their attention was on her, not on each other. She sensed no jealous rivalry from Jason at all. Just enthusiasm.

"Take your time, Dinosaur Lady."

"Whenever you're ready, Noelle."

Noelle took in a deep breath. She'd *never* be ready, but that was beside the point. It was now or never. She gulped in a second deep breath, tightened her grasp on Matt's shoulders and slipped her right foot into the empty stirrup. She boosted herself up, and before she knew it, she was mounted.

"You did it!" Jason beamed. "You're actually on a horse!"

"Now," Matt went on, "gently kick your foot out of the stirrup so I can put mine back in."

She gingerly slid her foot back.

"Scoot closer and hold on to my waist with both hands. Don't worry about the saddlebags. And don't be afraid to get a good grip on me."

Noelle did as she was told, her attention on Matt, then on the horse. But when the animal shifted its weight from one leg to another, throwing her against Matt's hard back, her attention suddenly shifted. The tingling response of her own physical attraction made her gasp.

"Are you okay?" both Matt and Jason immediately asked.

"Ummm, yeah," Noelle said, sliding farther back. "It's just that I can *feel* him under me," Noelle improvised.

The horse moved again, and she gulped.

"His muscles are moving! And he's—he's warm!" It was a curious sensation. She could feel the horse's body heat right through her jeans legs. Just like she could feel Matt's body heat against her arms.

"Horses are warm-blooded mammals, just like us," Matt reminded her.

She could certainly attest to that. Her own body was *definitely* feeling warm.

She felt the powerful flank flex again, causing Matt's ribs to shift beneath her fingers. "This is so... different."

In more ways than one.

"Then we'll just stand here until you're comfortable. Tell me when you're ready to go."

Matt's nearness was doing strange things to her. Noelle deliberately forced her thoughts to Jason.

"I guess I'm as ready as I'll ever be. You—you won't run him or jump him without telling me, will you?"

"We'll ride nice and slow. You have my word, Noelle. Here we go."

Matt clicked his tongue, and the horse moved forward in a slow walk. Noelle wasn't aware she was holding her breath until Matt said, "Breathe, Noelle. You don't want to get light-headed."

But it wasn't holding her breath that made her feel light-headed. It was Matt's touch, his nearness, his body's strength beneath her fingertips. Her own body was more aware of Matt than of the massive horse beneath her, and for the life of her she didn't know if that was good or not.

Noelle tightened her grip around his waist again. Even though the horse was walking, they were covering an awful lot of ground in a very short time.

"Noelle?"

"Horses sure move fast, don't they?" she asked in an attempt to be humorous. She bit her lip as they approached a branched-off loop of the old creek bed. That shallow hole seemed awfully formidable from atop the horse.

Matt reined the stallion to a halt. "We have to cross the creek bed here. You go first, Jason. I'm going to let Dr. Forrest off here. I think she's had enough riding for today."

Ain't that the truth, Noelle silently agreed. She loosened her grip on Matt's waist as Jason said, "Dr. Forrest, grab your—"

She turned toward him, just in time to see a trowel slip out of her half-opened backpack pocket. It bounced off the horse's flank, catching everyone by surprise, including Matt. He was half turned in the saddle to help her dismount. Then everything happened at once. The horse kicked and bucked, and Noelle sailed through the air.

Before she knew it, she was facedown in the dirt, just as Jason's wild yell caused the horse to rear. Concerned for Jason, she immediately rolled over and opened her eyes. But her gaze didn't fasten on Jason; it was locked on the hooves directly above her—the same hooves that were descending fast. In a purely instinctive movement she covered her head with her arms and rolled rapidly out of the way.

The horse landed just inches from her head. And then, as quickly as it had begun, the crisis was over. Matt had the huge animal under control and backing away from her. He was dismounting even as Noelle sat up and wiped the dirt from her bleeding mouth.

She saw Jason, and wondered if her own face was as white as his.

"I'm all right, sweetheart," she said immediately.

But her voice was shaky, and her legs weren't much better. She decided to remain sitting on the ground awhile longer.

Matt tied his horse to a nearby tree and hurried to her side. And Jason, with no help from anyone, had dismounted, too, and was frantically untying his crutches.

Matt knelt beside her, his hands on her shoulders.

"Are you okay?" he asked. His voice was calm, but his face was pale under its tan.

"I'm fine. Just . . . a bit shaken, that's all."

He ran his hands over her arms and legs. "No pain anywhere? Sure you aren't hurt?"

Noelle nodded and tried to control the excitement that surged through her when she felt his touch, brisk and matter-of-fact though it was. "At the risk of sounding clichéd, the only thing hurt is my pride. Which goeth before a fall, if I remember correctly."

She tried to smile. And failed miserably.

"No broken bones," Matt announced, finishing with his examination.

"Told you so." She tucked up her legs and wrapped her shaking arms around her dusty jeans.

Matt pulled a handkerchief out of his pocket and carefully wiped her face. "Your lip's bleeding." He positioned her hand over the hanky and said, "Hold this right here."

Noelle probed her cut lip with her tongue. As cuts went, it wasn't a bad one. "Matt, would you go help Jason before he ends up in the dirt himself? Look at him."

Matt turned. Jason was determinedly making his way over the rough terrain toward them.

"Jason, I told you I'm fine," Noelle called to him. "You don't have to come."

Jason said nothing and kept moving, slowly and hesitantly. But Matt didn't leave her side.

"Matt, go help him!"

"Not until I know you're okay. You look like hell."

"Forget about me! Go get Jason!"

Dear lord, please don't let that boy fall, Noelle prayed. She watched with her heart in her throat.

"Jason's fine, Noelle." Matt looked from her to the boy with a strange expression. "I don't think I should leave you. If you were really okay, you'd be up on your feet by now— and running over to him."

"I would, but I, uh, need to catch my breath first." In truth, she was afraid she'd faint. Her hand fell from her lip and the hanky dropped to the ground.

She heard Matt swear, then he was gently pushing her head between her knees. "Deep breaths before you pass out."

It helped. "And I thought live TV was bad," she sighed.

"So instead you climbed up on a horse—something that obviously terrifies you—because of an eleven-year-old boy?"

"I never said I was terrified," she retorted with a ghost of her old spirit. "Like I told you, I'm just a little nervous around big hooves and huge teeth. Besides, if Jason can show an interest in my work, the least I can do is act interested in horses."

"You really care about Jason, don't you?"

She lifted her head. "That's what I've been telling you all along! I have only Jason's best interests at heart," she said with exasperation. *The man's skull was almost as thick as any dinosaur's!* "Of course, I never would have done it if I'd known you owned such a wild bronco."

"Just…save your air and keep breathing. Keep the head down."

Noelle obeyed. After a few more minutes the dizziness passed, and she carefully lifted her head. The second she did, a waiting Jason threw his arms around her, buried his face in her shoulder and held on tight.

"Oh, Jason, I'm so sorry I frightened you." Noelle drew him into her lap, braces and all, and gently smoothed back his hair. "I didn't mean to fall off, sweetheart."

Jason said nothing, but his body was shaking almost as badly as hers had earlier.

Noelle looked toward Matt, hoping for some help. But Matt was busy picking up the bloodied hanky, then her trowel. He walked over to her backpack and placed both in an unzipped pocket, which he fastened safely.

Jason raised his face to hers. "I tried to tell you, Dinosaur Lady. I saw it slip out. Are you okay?"

Noelle nodded. She was glad to see the color coming back into the boy's cheeks. "I must not have zipped the tool pocket. It was all my fault."

But Matt shook his head. "It's okay, Noelle. It was an accident—and accidents happen."

Matt wasn't going to blame her?

"Thank goodness you aren't hurt. Keep calm and save your breath."

Noelle was more than happy to comply. She silently watched as Matt helped Jason to his feet and got him back up on his pony.

"You wait here," he ordered. He untied his own horse, now greatly calmed. Reins in hand, Matt led him away from the tree. "I'll go back and get the Jeep."

"There's no need," she insisted. "I'm okay." And to prove it, she got to her own feet unaided. "See? I can walk."

"I'll walk with you, then."

"No!" she cried. She took a quick step backward, safely away from Matt's horse. "Keep away!"

Matt froze so abruptly the horse's nose hit him in the back.

"Please, you just mount up and go on ahead," Noelle begged. "Far, far ahead, okay?"

Matt stared at her for the longest time. Then he said in a strange voice, "Whatever you want. But if you need anything, I'll be within calling distance. Jason, keep an eye on her for me, okay?"

"I will," Jason promised. Finally Matt turned and mounted, then started toward the stables. Noelle and Jason were left to trail along behind, Noelle keeping her distance from even the little pony Jason rode.

"You shouldn't have told Matt to leave!" Jason blurted out.

"But Jason, I honestly can't help it if I don't like horses any more than Matt likes dinosaurs."

"You didn't tell the horse to leave. You told *Matt* to leave."

Noelle's heart twisted at the rare censure in Jason's face. Funny how much the opinion of one little boy was beginning to mean to her. They walked in silence, Matt still ahead of them.

"I think Matt likes you," Jason added. "It wouldn't hurt you to like him back."

"Like him back?"

"Yes. You aren't very nice to him sometimes."

Noelle watched Matt turn in the saddle from time to time to check on their progress, then watched Jason's troubled face. She sighed. Now she had *two* miserable males on her hands.

"Sweetheart, let me explain something to you. The fact that you found that fossil and gave it to me was a real miracle. My getting permission to search for more fossils on Matt's land was the second miracle. I'm not here to make Matt like me. I'm here to make my peers respect me. This could be my big break—my one-in-a-million chance to make a name for myself."

"But you already have a name for yourself!" Jason insisted. "You're the Dinosaur Lady!"

Noelle could have screamed. How could she tell Jason the real facts of her professional life without upsetting him?

"Jason, I need more dig work. And I need more museum time. My peers don't consider the 'Dinosaur Lady' a real paleontologist."

"You *are* a real one!" he said fiercely. "You *are!*"

Noelle's throat tightened at his loyalty. "Yes, I am," she said after a minute. "And I love doing *Fun with Fossils,* just as much as I love—" she started to say *you,* then thought better of it "—working with kids like you. *Especially* you. The best part about your fossil, Jason, was that you came with it.

"But in the real world of paleontology, I'm—well, let's just say I don't have much of a name for myself. I'm affiliated with a private museum that has no stars, a small collection of fossils and an even smaller reputation. Being on television isn't going to get me out of there and into a prestigious museum."

"Like Denver's Museum of Natural History?"

"Exactly."

"Well, *I* think you're good enough to get in, even if they don't."

"I do, too, Jason," she said seriously. "But unless I can prove it to *them,* it'll never happen. I'll only be handling plaster replicas of other people's discoveries, instead of discovering them myself. I simply have to concentrate on my career."

"But what about Matt?"

"That's what I'm trying to explain, Jason. Matt and I don't agree about this." Noelle looked off in the distance at Matt's retreating figure. "I can't give up my fossil hunting just to make him happy."

No matter how much she was beginning to wish she could....

CHAPTER SIX

FOR THE NEXT FEW DAYS, Noelle had sore muscles and bruises that reminded her of the horseback fiasco. Not that she needed any extra reminders when confronted with Matt's polite coolness and Alex's bitter silence.

She'd finally met Alex Caldwell at a belated dinner with a quiet Matt and subdued Jason. She'd been in for a shock, and the fact that Alex had a cane and serious leg deformities was the least of it.

Unfair, even irrational though it was, Noelle's gut instinct was that Alex's personality was as twisted as his body. She was immediately ashamed of her first reaction and tried to compensate by being extra-friendly to Alex.

It wasn't easy. Alex wasn't much of a "people person." Noelle soon realized that Jason didn't like Alex, either. She also knew that most children had a built-in radar when it came to adults, and Jason was especially bright.

"Didn't Matt tell you about me?" Alex had asked in a snide tone.

"I knew he had a brother," she'd replied, "and that you were out of town on a buying trip. Nothing more."

"Matt always was the strong, silent type," Alex had said with a mocking smile. There was an edge to his voice, almost malicious, that had bothered her. No wonder Jason kept his distance.

"I'm afraid I'm not strong anymore—or silent—thanks to the plane crash." Alex had taken in Noelle's startled look. "Or didn't Matt tell you about all those gory details, either? How about it, Jason? Want to hear the whole story?"

Jason shifted uncomfortably in his chair. Noelle noticed that his meal was untouched. Not that she blamed him. Alex seemed to have a way of ruining everyone's appetite—including hers. After the earlier trauma with the horse, this was the last thing she or Jason needed. And Matt, unfortunately, had stepped out of the kitchen to take a business phone call.

"Jason, why don't you go to your room and finish cleaning up?" she suggested, even though she knew he had. "And here." She pressed a plum and some cookies into his hand. "Take these in case you get hungry later."

Jason gave her a grateful smile, stuffed them in his pockets and was gone as fast as his crutches could carry him. Alex followed his retreat, then turned cold eyes on Noelle.

"What's wrong, Dr. Forrest? Afraid to let the boy hear about the cruel facts of life?"

"Oh, I think Jason is fully aware of those. He doesn't need any more lessons." She gave Alex a tight smile. "If anyone needs them, I'd say it was you, starting with table manners and not upsetting young boys. Next time, why don't you harass someone who can fight back?" *Like me,* her expression clearly said. "It would be much more sporting."

Alex flushed at her words, not from embarrassment, she sensed, but from anger. His eyes narrowed, and Noelle instantly knew she'd made an enemy.

"You're not his mother," he spat out.

"I am while he's in this house," she shot back, much to Alex's astonishment. "And if I ever see you deliberately upsetting Jason again, I'll—"

"That's enough, both of you!" Matt curtly ordered. "I leave the room for five minutes and come back to this? What's going on?"

"Noelle feels our parents' death was too upsetting a topic for Jason. I was just disagreeing, and she flew at me like a mother hen, claws and all."

Now it was Noelle's turn to flush. Alex wasn't the only one she'd surprised with her fierce outburst. She'd astonished herself—and insulted Matt's brother in the process, in his own home, no less. Furthermore, she knew she'd stick up for Jason in a second, fossils or no fossils. Luckily, Matt took her side.

"Alex, she's right. Leave Jason alone. If you want to talk about our past, do so away from my guests and the kitchen table. And make sure you leave out the 'gory details,'" he ordered.

"Since you don't like *my* version, why don't you tell her?" Alex muttered.

There was an expression on Matt's face, a look of weary resignation, that Noelle had never seen before. Immediately she said, "Matt, you don't have to tell me anything. Why don't I go check on Jason?"

She'd started to rise from her chair, but Matt motioned her back down.

"No, it's okay. You might as well hear. It's common knowledge, anyway." He closed his eyes briefly. "When my father was alive, our ranch had a plane. Dad had a pilot's license, and he was always taking out-of-town trips to make purchases. The plane was hit by lightning during a bad storm."

"Oh, Matt! How awful!"

"Yes . . . Only Alex survived."

"I didn't walk away, though," Alex said bitterly. "Can you believe it? Usually Dad went alone, but this time Mom and I came along for the ride."

Matt rested one hand on his brother's shoulder. "Alex sustained some pretty bad pelvic and leg fractures."

"Wrong, brother dear. You mean, 'Alex suffered major deformities caused by shattered legs and hips.'"

Matt didn't correct him. "I'm afraid there wasn't much salvageable bone left to mend. Alex was in a wheelchair for a long time. He still needs a cane to get around."

"I'm so sorry to hear that. It must have been awful for you, Alex. For both of you."

"I'm just grateful that Alex survived. And that he recovered enough to be mobile," Matt said quietly.

Alex gave his brother a scathing look. "If you want to call it that." He pushed away from the table and, grabbing his cane, limped away.

Noelle watched him leave in silence. Finally she said, "That is one very angry man."

Matt quickly leapt to Alex's defense. "Usually he has better control of himself."

"I'm glad to hear it. I'd hate to think Alex was like this around the patients."

"No. He usually blows off steam when the two of us are alone."

"It's too bad Jason was the exception. I should probably go check on him now."

As she stood up, Matt reached for her arm. "Let me go talk with Jason and apologize for my brother. Then I'll speak to Alex. That should smooth things out."

"I don't know, Matt," Noelle said uneasily. "I have a feeling it's going to take more than that. And you shouldn't apologize for Alex. He's old enough to do that himself."

Matt sighed and released her arm. "I wouldn't hold my breath waiting for an apology, Noelle. Alex hasn't really made peace with himself since the plane crash."

"You mean he hasn't accepted his disabilities. Matt, has he even tried?"

"It's hard for him. Alex was never really very flexible, even as a boy. He hates change."

"But Matt, how can he deny what's happened to him? He has to live with his injuries every day!"

"I know." Sorrow flickered in Matt's eyes. "What happened to Alex was too much too fast. His emotional system overloaded. And it wasn't just the accident, either," Matt inserted when Noelle would have spoken. "Alex lost his parents, his health and his job."

"How long ago was his accident, Matt?"

"Ten years. Alex was fifteen at the time."

"Ten years! Matt, after ten years, don't you think it's time Alex *did* accept it all?"

"Of course it is! Don't you think I've tried to help him?" Matt ran his fingers through his hair. "I went back to school. I became a recreational therapist especially for Alex. I started this ranch for riders with special needs, and taught Alex to ride again. Then I made sure he had a job where he could feel useful." Matt gestured toward the window, where the riding rings and neat paddocks were visible. "What more can I do?"

Maybe you did too much. Maybe you should have let Alex fight his own battles, she thought. "Have you ever considered getting Alex emotional help?" she asked softly.

"As in psychiatrist?"

"Why not? I've only just met Alex, but even I can see that he needs someone to talk to."

"I've suggested counseling. Alex refuses."

"Did he give a reason?"

"Money, for one."

"Money? But . . . Matt, I don't understand."

"Alex was one of those unfortunate people I told you about who fell through the private insurance cracks." Matt's lips twisted unpleasantly. "Our former carrier canceled Alex's health insurance years ago. I pay cash for any medical care he needs."

No wonder Matt is lobbying so hard for a national health care system, Noelle realized. Her heart went out to him and his brother.

"Good lord, Matt, in addition to everything else, Alex's care could have bankrupted you! Instead of losing just your parents, you both could have lost your home!"

"We almost did," Matt said grimly. "But that's beside the point. If Alex ever consented to therapy, I'd sell every inch of land I own if I had to. But he refuses. He says it's too costly and that he already has me to talk to."

Noelle shook her head. "You're hardly an objective listener, Matt."

"I disagree. I understand more than anyone what Alex went through. They were my parents, too."

Noelle reached across the table for his hand. "Matt, I'm so sorry about that. But if I were Alex, the last person I'd want to confide in is the one family member lucky enough *not* to have been on that plane."

"That's not true!" Matt pulled his hand away. "Alex and I are very close."

For the first time ever, she saw his control slip and decided to tread carefully.

"Perhaps I'm wrong. But he still needs counseling. Maybe he'd get it if you'd stop being so...tolerant."

Suddenly the hardness was back in his eyes. "You're blaming Alex's behavior on me?"

"A part of it, yes," she said bluntly. "Matt, you're in a medical profession. You know what an enabler is. Whether it's alcohol, drugs or mental problems, you don't help by tolerating unacceptable behavior. And Alex's behavior is not normal."

Matt rose. From the furious look on his face, Noelle knew she'd gone too far.

"I don't need any advice on how to help my family. And if I did, I'd get it from someone who prefers the *living* over the dead."

His words stabbed at her heart. When Matt left, Noelle hadn't gone after him.

A chilly silence had swept over the house after the evening meal. Fortunately, Jason's good mood had returned the following morning. Unfortunately, neither Matt's nor Alex's did. Not that day, nor in the days to come. One afternoon, midway through the second week, Noelle even went so far as to suggest that Jason consider cutting his visit short.

"I'm not leaving unless Matt says I have to." Jason's chin set in determination. "Besides, Matt made Alex say he was sorry," he added. "Matt said he wouldn't bother us anymore."

Noelle wasn't so certain. Already Alex had driven a wedge between her and Matt. Not that she needed any help with that, she thought ruefully. Matt and the fossils were a bad combination to start with. Alex had only made it worse.

Matt had remained—not exactly cool around her—but quiet. She suspected he was counting the days until she left. With only a week and a half to go, she supposed she couldn't expect anything else. Why, then, was she so disappointed?

The next day, Thursday of the second week, it was with mixed emotions that she passed over her jeans and cotton shirt, and dressed in her working outfit of skirt, blouse and blazer. She had a taping of *Fun with Fossils* this morning, plus she needed to get to the museum's computer. Jason was coming with her.

Everyone was at the breakfast table when she walked in— even Alex. Noelle greeted them all, relieved to see that Jason was just about finished. At least Alex hadn't ruined *this* meal for him.

"Good morning, Noelle. Do you want anything to eat?" Matt asked her. "Maybe some coffee?"

His request was polite, but neutral. Noelle couldn't tell if she was still out of grace with him or not. However, there was no uncertainty where Alex was concerned. After his glacial "Good morning," Alex didn't say another word to her.

"No thanks, Matt." She didn't even set down her brief-case. "I'll grab something later."

"You're all dressed up," he observed. "No digging today?"

"No. I have to be at the studio by nine. I'm doing another taping of *Fun with Fossils*. After that, I have to run over to the museum to use my computer. Jason will be coming with me. Right, kiddo?"

"Right, Dinosaur Lady. I'm ready when you are." Jason gave her a big grin.

She rumpled the boy's hair, then on a sudden impulse kissed his cheek. No matter how low her spirits were, Jason always made things brighter. Too bad her charm didn't seem to work around adults the way it did with children. Just once it would be nice to see Matt light up like Jason did when she walked into a room.

"I have a computer you could use," Matt offered. "We only need it for billing and accounts at the end of the month."

The offer actually sounded genuine. Was Matt making a peace offering? If so, it was a shame she'd have to disappoint him.

"Thanks, Matt, but I doubt it has the software I need. My computer ties into the museum's mainframe. It has a special program that converts flat topographical maps and other input into three-dimensional overlays. Those can help target any potential fossil sites. I have enough information from here to give it a shot."

"I see. Well, keep me posted. Come on, Jason. I'll walk you and Noelle out to the car."

"I'll walk her to the car myself," Jason insisted. He deliberately stood up and took Noelle's briefcase into one hand.

"Why, thank you, Jason."

Alex morosely watched him balance crutches and briefcase. "Aren't you the little gentleman."

Both Noelle and Jason pretended to not to hear him, which seemed to be the best defense against Alex's frequent snide remarks. "Come on, Dinosaur Lady," Jason said. "We don't want to be late for the show."

"You're awfully quiet, Jason," Noelle said later. They were a good half hour into their drive to the city. "You've barely said a word during the ride."

"Alex makes me so mad! I hate him!" Jason exploded.

Noelle frowned, searching for the right words. "I know he's annoying sometimes. But Jason, Alex Caldwell is very unhappy. We shouldn't hate someone because he's unhappy."

Jason refused to be mollified. "Well, I do! Matt's in a bad mood, you're upset, and it's all Alex's fault! He's ruining everything!"

"Sweetheart, he hasn't ruined *everything*. Matt will calm down eventually. And I'm fine. I could never be anything but fine when I'm with you," Noelle said with a coaxing smile.

There was no favorable response from Jason. "Alex hates it when people are happy," he grumbled. "What if he tells you lies about me, Dinosaur Lady? What if he says I'm bad? Grown-ups always believe other grown-ups over kids. What if you never want to see me again?"

Jason lifted a worried face to hers. With her free hand she reached for his. Jason's fingers curled around hers and held on tight.

"Jason, I'd always believe you over Alex. I promise you, kiddo, nothing he does or says can hurt us. *Ever.*"

"How can you be so sure, Dr. Forrest?" To Noelle's horror, Jason looked as if he was about to cry.

"Because I love you too much to let it happen."

The words just slipped out, but to Noelle, they felt so right as she spoke them to the boy beside her.

"Love is much stronger than anger or hate. Alex doesn't know that, Jason. But *I* know."

"You—you're not worried?"

"No."

"Alex can't make you hate me? Or Matt, either?"

"*Never.* I'm one tough customer. And so is Matt. So don't you worry, sweetheart, okay?"

Jason ducked his head, but he didn't pull his hand out of hers. Noelle was content to remain silent, continuing her drive into the city. When Jason finally lifted his face again, Noelle was pleased to see that most of his worry was gone.

"Feel better now?"

"Some. Do you think Alex ever will ever stop being so...so mean?"

"Maybe some day. Matt said Alex has a hard time accepting change."

"Alex is so stupid," Jason said with some of his old spirit. "He wants everything to go back to the way it was before his accident. But it never will. Wishing for it will just make you crazy. I know."

Noelle caught her breath at Jason's words. They revealed an insight, a maturity beyond his years. "It does?"

Jason nodded. "I told Alex only stupid people believed wishing would make something come true. It was like when I was in the hospital. I kept wishing for my legs to work right. I didn't want a wheelchair because that meant I'd never get my wish. Finally I just quit being stupid. I mean, I couldn't find any fossils lying around in bed, now, could I?"

"No, I guess not." Noelle couldn't believe Jason's frank honesty. "And you told Alex all this?"

"Yeah, when I first started riding at Matt's. I said I knew he was waiting for some miracle. Just like on TV or something. And that was so dumb."

Noelle bit her lip. No wonder Alex disliked Jason. He was the harsh voice of reality. "I don't think Alex is ready to listen to what you have to say, Jason."

"He'll never be ready," Jason said disdainfully.

"Alex will eventually have to come to terms with his life on his own. Just like you did. I want you to leave Alex alone. Just stay away from him, okay?"

"I already do. I'm just glad you and Matt aren't letting Alex bother us anymore."

He sighed contentedly, then released Noelle's hand to fiddle with the radio. In a few minutes a Denver rock-and-roll station was blaring through the car speakers.

Noelle made no move to turn down the volume. In truth, she welcomed the chance to digest what she'd just heard. Jason could very well be right about Alex. If Alex refused to acknowledge his injuries because he was waiting for a miracle... With his fragile illusions, Alex Caldwell was a walking time bomb. Anything could set him off, especially a major change in his life.

Such as Matt dating Connie. Even though Alex had nothing to do with the fact that Matt and Connie had gone their separate ways, the situation could have become explosive. And what about Matt's future? Surely Alex couldn't expect Matt to remain alone the rest of his life. What if Matt let another woman into his life? *What if that woman was Noelle herself?*

All right, so he wasn't in love with her. But she *was* on his ranch searching for fossils; what if she actually found them? Would that send Alex over the edge, ruining Noelle in the process?

And what about Jason? Jason adored Matt almost as much as he idolized Noelle. Matt was fond of Jason, too—but unlike Alex, Jason wasn't his brother. When it came to taking sides, how could Jason compete with Alex for Matt's loyalty? The child could very well get caught in the crossfire.

The situation at the ranch was fraught with pitfalls. If only she'd met Matt under different circumstances! Noelle sighed heavily. When it came to her chances with Matt, she might as well be shooting dice. There were so many uncertainties—except for one.

Alex Caldwell was headed for a fall. She only prayed he didn't take anyone with him.

She tried to put aside her worries and fears as she prepared to tape her show. Fortunately, Jason Reilly stepped on stage for his promised second round as guest co-host. If it weren't for Jason's stage presence and enthusiastic, spontaneous responses, Noelle suspected her discouragement might have affected her performance.

It was incredible that a fostered child with a father in prison, a mother who'd abandoned him, and a permanent disability could be so cheerful. Noelle felt ashamed of her own despondent behavior and was determined to snap out of it. She forced herself to go through her script with a smile.

Finally the taping was almost over. She breathed a sigh of relief as the cameras' red lights went out and the director yelled, "That's a wrap!"

"How'd we do?" Jason asked eagerly.

"*You* did fine," Noelle replied. "I've done better."

"Oh, no. You were perfect!"

Noelle smiled at the boy's loyalty. "I wasn't, but thanks, anyway, Jason," Noelle said with real affection. "Now we'd better get over to the museum."

Somehow her hand found its way to Jason's shoulder. Together they strolled toward the studio's parking garage, and Jason gallantly opened her car door. Noelle drove them through downtown and east toward the foothills where the Colorado Museum of Paleontology was located.

"Instead of using the staff back entrance, shall we take the long way through the exhibits?" Noelle suggested. "There are some new displays just up." CMP did have some beautiful displays. Whole authentic skeletons were rare and valuable, but CMP had obtained realistic plaster duplicates. Noelle hungered for the Denver Museum of Natural

History's authentic displays, but she suspected that Jason wouldn't mind. She was right.

"That would be great!" Jason's eyes shone with excitement.

They strolled through the spacious areas holding the reproductions of the latest discoveries. Or rather, Noelle strolled. Despite his crutches, Jason forged eagerly ahead, darting from one exhibit to the next.

"There's *Supersaurus!*" Jason pointed. "And *Ultrasaurus,* too."

"Yep, that Jim Jensen is one lucky man," Noelle said, fighting against the purely unprofessional stab of envy inside her.

Both new species had been discovered by Colorado's famous Jim Jensen. Not only had he made numerous major fossil discoveries in the state, he'd discovered the remains of previously unknown dinosaur species.

"Yeah, but he doesn't have his own TV show," Jason said. With his tossed-off words, he dismissed the accomplishments of a man so famous his name was a household word among paleontologists. "Not like you."

Noelle allowed herself a brief flush of pleasure before saying, "Come on, my office is next on the tour. Follow me."

However, there was more on the tour than just her office. Someone was waiting outside her door.

"Matt? Look, Dr. Forrest, it's Matt!"

"So it is." His presence did strange things to her insides. Her emotional gauge zipped past pleased to downright happy. "Hello, Matt," she managed to say in a casual manner. "This is a nice surprise. We didn't expect to see you here."

"I had a few cancellations, and one of the therapists wanted some overtime. The studio told me you'd be here. I thought I'd take you and Jason out to lunch."

"We'd like that." Noelle smiled. "But I need to finish up here first. I was just about to hit the computer. Come on in."

"This is a *neat* office," Jason remarked a few moments later. Noelle watched the other two take in the numerous molds and casts of fossils. Jason gave a slow whistle of appreciation. Matt's enthusiasm wasn't as great, but if he had any negative thoughts, he was keeping them to himself.

"Where's the fossil Jason found?" Matt asked curiously.

"One of the other paleontologists is working on it." Noelle crossed to her desk and booted up her computer.

"Why don't *you* get to clean it?" Jason asked, twirling a whisk brush in his fingers.

Noelle hated hearing the obvious question, but answered it, anyway.

"Usually a paleontologist has rights to a fossil only if he or she makes the initial discovery. You were the one who unearthed the find, not me. The moment you announced on my show that you were donating it to the museum, I had to turn it over to my boss."

"That's not fair! I wanted *you* to have it!"

"And I would have loved keeping it." Noelle sighed. "But since there were no landowner claims from Matt, I had no choice."

Matt studied her carefully. "Why?"

"The museum feels I don't have enough field experience to handle a new find. So the fossil went to someone with more seniority."

"How will you ever get the experience if they don't let you work on it in the first place? You shouldn't put up with it, Dinosaur Lady!" Jason slapped her desk with the palm of his hand for emphasis.

Matt agreed. "It seems like a no-win situation to me."

"That's the fossil biz," Noelle said lightly, but she couldn't help feeling touched by their sympathy. Even though she hadn't said anything to family or friends, it *had* been hard to give up Jason's fossil—far harder than anyone had realized.

"Did they ever determine what dinosaur that fossil came from?" Matt wondered.

"No, the museum is still checking. The fossil was that of a juvenile beast, which makes it hard to categorize by size. And the bone was not only weathered, it was fragmented and incomplete, which complicates matters. We need to find the bed it came from."

"Cheer up, Dinosaur Lady," Jason said encouragingly. "I just know if there's more fossils to be found, you'll find them."

"Maybe..." Noelle's voice trailed off. Her earlier concerns about what might happen if she discovered fossils on Matt's ranch returned, and she made an effort to shake them off. She sat down to key up her 3-D map program on the computer.

"Come over here, guys, and I'll demonstrate how this works. Let's see..."

She hesitated a moment, then typed in a location code— one that wasn't Matt's ranch. Perhaps she could sway Matt to her point of view if she used a more neutral example.

"First I'll show Jason what I'm working on for my next show," Noelle announced. "The topic's going to be the Morrison Formation."

Matt nodded his understanding. Like just about every resident of Colorado, he was familiar with the Morrison Formation and its rich fossil bed.

"Exactly what aspect of the Morrison are you going to concentrate on?" He pulled up a chair and sat next to Noelle in front of the monitor. On her other side, Jason did the same.

"Well, most local children know *what* it is and *where* it is. But that isn't enough. I want them to know *why* it's here." She gestured toward the computer. "I thought some diagrams would help. So I'm making up maps to use for display purposes."

Jason pointed toward blue areas on the monitor. "What are these?" he asked curiously.

"Those are computer-generated water flows—Precambrian shallow seas and Mesozoic lakes that once covered Colorado." She keyed the sequence that brought up the 3-D display of present-day Colorado. "This is our state today. The original floodplains were approximately here."

Her fingers danced over the computer keys as she overlaid the two maps.

"And here, along the front range, is the Morrison Formation." Noelle highlighted the area in green. "See? I want to show the direct cause-and-effect relationship between the floodplains then and our fossil beds today."

Matt studied her overlay carefully. "I know most fossil finds *are* found in the Morrison Formation."

"Or along the banks of the Green and Yampa rivers in Dinosaur National Park," Jason added.

"That's correct. Those rivers, along with the Colorado, have been here since the Cenozoic era."

"My ranch is nowhere near either of those areas," he remarked. "And my shallow little creek certainly didn't originate from prehistoric times."

"Probably not. But nothing's one-hundred percent sure in this business."

"Theoretically there shouldn't be any fossils on my property."

"That's not necessarily true. There are always exceptions to the rule. You can still find fossils on unlikely pockets of land."

"Like your ranch, Matt."

"That's right, Jason." Noelle made a few more adjustments to her map, then saved the program to disk. She then typed in the sequence for the file on Matt's ranch and called it up on the screen.

"I can't understand why you're making such a fuss over what—in your own words—probably isn't even a whole skeleton," Matt said.

"Even small pieces of fossils are welcome finds," Noelle insisted. "Every bit of knowledge we gain from every single find, no matter how insignificant, is valuable!"

"And every single gain my patients make—every small step of confidence and independence they take—is valuable, too."

Noelle could see where this conversation was headed.

"Here, Jason. You take my chair and study the 3-D lay-out. Matt and I are going outside for a minute."

"How come?" he asked.

"I'm thirsty," she improvised. "We're going to get some sodas from the machine. What kind do you want?"

"Root beer, please," he said, his attention already on the computer as she and Matt stepped outside.

"I hope you didn't drive all the way down here to argue with me in front of Jason," Noelle told him bluntly.

"No. To tell you the truth, I drove all the way down here to spend some time with you."

"Me?"

"You needn't look so surprised," Matt said with the barest trace of irritation. "Since you brought Jason along, I didn't think I'd be interrupting your work. In fact, I'd ac-tually been hoping you'd include me in your invitation."

Pleased at his admission, yet somewhat confused, Noelle searched for words as she led Matt down the hall to the vending machines in the staff lounge. "I didn't mean to be rude. But you knew I was coming here today," she de-fended herself, "and you didn't seem very interested in joining us. Usually you see red every time I bring up my oc-cupation."

"No, I see red every time you dismiss *mine*."

"I'm not saying my work is more important than yours," she said through gritted teeth. "By the same token, I'm not saying your work is more important than mine."

Matt froze in his tracks. "How can you even suggest that?"

"You needn't look so shocked. It's all a question of pri-orities." She stopped to face him. "I remember years ago when I was a child and the Apollo moon project was un-derway. Protestors screamed that the money invested in putting a man on the moon should be used for the poor and homeless instead."

"Good causes, surely."

"Of course they were. They still are. But Matt, the quest for knowledge can't take a back seat to the world's trage-dies! I try to teach children that knowledge is power. Only knowledge will ultimately cure the world's problems. The moon project is an excellent example. Because of the information gained by NASA, we now have an excellent satellite communications system. People can call for help from anywhere in the world."

"That doesn't necessarily mean they'll get it," Matt contended.

"True, but at least they can ask! At least they'll be heard! Earthquake and flood victims, even victims of war, have the voice of the world now. Disaster victims can call for help immediately, all because someone had the courage to search for knowledge."

Matt's eyes narrowed. "That's small consolation to a starving child, but I'll concede your point. However, I don't see how digging up some long-dead remains can possibly stand up against my patients' welfare, or the national health care system they so desperately need."

"Can't you? Matt, the dinosaurs are a clear-cut example of a thriving, healthy race that suddenly, completely died out. That very same thing is happening to our plant and animal life today! And to *us!* If ever there was a race bent on self-destruction, it's the human race." Noelle shivered at the thought. "That's why dinosaurs hold such a universal appeal. Even children realize that these mighty life forms should have been indestructible. But they weren't. And neither are we!"

"This search to know what happened to the dinosaurs—what you're saying is that everyone has a personal stake in it?" Matt said slowly.

"Exactly! That's why discovering what happened to them is so important! If it could happen to the strongest of the strong, it could happen to us. Many nations don't care if razing the rain forests upsets the weather patterns. Or if pollution destroys our ionosphere. Or if nuclear reactors poison our water and soil. But if we discover that the dinosaurs died from these same causes—disruptions in weather, say—only triggered by natural instead of man-made conditions, then whole countries might realize it could happen to us. And do something about it!"

"And you honestly think that could happen?" He sounded skeptical again.

"Yes! Paleontology is one of the few scientific fields where knowledge isn't jealously guarded like...like military secrets! Think about it, Matt. *Everyone* wants to know what happened to the dinosaurs, from paleontologists like me to kids like Jason. If we can ever find out the real reason they disappeared, perhaps—just perhaps—we'll fight harder to save ourselves."

There was silence in the hall. Then Matt spoke. "I'm sorry, but I see too many of life's harsh realities day after day. I don't have much room left for crazy idealists."

"Is that what you think I am?" She ignored the ache in her stomach. "A crazy idealist with even crazier dreams?"

Matt spread his hands, palms outward. "What else would you call it? You spend your life searching, researching and digging for the dead. How can I applaud forever looking backward?"

"I don't know why not," was Noelle's stinging reply. "You let Alex do just that."

CHAPTER SEVEN

"THAT'S A DAMN LIE!"

"Is it, Matt? Is it really?"

"You leave Alex out of this!"

"I can't! Not when Alex is why you're so prejudiced against fossil hunting. The only reason you tolerate me is because I'm finding you sponsors!"

"Let's hope you are," he ground out. "That's the only thing keeping you on my ranch!"

"You'll get your money," she retorted. "But all the money in the world can't buy a miracle for your brother. It won't help him put the past behind him. The sooner he realizes that, the better."

Another staff worker walked down the hall, giving them a curious glance. Matt waited until the man had stepped into the staff lounge before answering. "Save your words of wisdom for your show biz family, Dinosaur Lady. Because when it comes to mine, you don't have a clue."

Noelle watched as he turned and left. She made her way back to her office without Matt.

"Matt couldn't stay," she explained unhappily.

"Was he mad?"

She nodded. It was easier than speaking with a lump in her throat. Matt had reached out to her for the first time in weeks, and she'd ruined things.

"He doesn't want us to find any fossils, does he?" Jason asked.

"No, sweetheart, I don't think he does."

Jason bit his lip. "But then why did he drive all the way down here? I don't understand."

"I think Matt wanted to come with us. I—I think I hurt his feelings when I didn't invite him. He drove down anyway... but he didn't stay long."

"Why? Did you chase him away again?"

"Not exactly, but..."

Suddenly it was all too much to explain to an eleven-year-old boy. Noelle sighed. "Just drink your soda, Jason."

STILL, IN SPITE OF Matt's obvious hostility, Noelle refused to cut back on her search. Every morning she and Jason left after breakfast to investigate possible dig sites. During the evenings she continued to do her phone work, soliciting pledge money while Jason read his dinosaur books or updated his journal.

Matt continued to join them in the evenings, chatting easily with Jason, playing the occasional game of cards with him, and being the perfect host to Noelle. He even helped her with the pledge paperwork from time to time. But once Jason left to get ready for bed, Matt went out to the stables and didn't come back.

With a painful heart, Noelle realized he didn't want to be alone with her. She had only the television for company, except for stray comments from Alex. Naturally his visits only occurred when Matt was nowhere nearby.

"Your three weeks are almost up, Dr. Forrest," he said one night. "It looks like you're going to be leaving empty-handed. Such a shame." His gloating tone belied his words.

Noelle refused to be baited. "I'm afraid my fossil search hasn't gone exactly the way I'd hoped," she replied. "But I still have a few days. Even if I don't find a thing, I've made some new friends in the process. I'm only sorry to have disrupted your household."

"I'll bet."

Yes, Alex usually managed to make her lonely evenings worse. Being rejected by Matt was painful enough, but being alone was infinitely preferable to being with the younger Caldwell. She wondered how Matt had managed to stand his brother's bitterness all these years.

Suddenly the walls seemed to be closing in on her. She had to get outside, away from Alex and his snide, vicious remarks. Noelle grabbed a sweater and strolled outside, taking the path that would lead her to the nearest paddock.

She leaned on the top rail of the fence and silently watched the horses settling down for the night. The evening breeze was cool and soothing; the sun was just setting behind the Rockies. The mountains with their late-summer foliage threw long shadows toward the east. One bold paint ambled up to the fence and pushed her head over the top rail. Noelle had ventured a few tentative pats on the silky neck when Matt found her.

"I thought you didn't like horses," he said quietly.

"They're beautiful animals. I've enjoyed being around them here at the ranch. Maybe I'll see about giving my oldest niece riding lessons. I think she'd enjoy it."

"But not you?" The mare remained a moment longer, then, when no treats were forthcoming, returned to the herd. "Or should I say, not with me?"

"You know, you have an uncanny knack for twisting my words around," she said, her voice unsteady. She moved away from the rail, intending to go back to the house.

"Then maybe you should stop talking," Matt said. He caught her retreating form with one strong arm and drew her close. "Maybe we *both* should."

His kiss was hard and fierce, yet behind that sudden fierceness was something else—an undeniable, surprising sweetness that welcomed Noelle even as it confused her. The kiss went on and on; it wasn't until Noelle pulled back that Matt released her.

She stared at him for the longest time, desperately trying to make sense out of what had happened, but failing. Finally she had to say something.

"What was that for?" she managed to get out.

Matt shoved his hands deep inside his jeans pockets. "Can't you tell?"

She shook her head. She thought she heard Matt sigh, but she wasn't sure.

"If you want, consider it a long-overdue apology. For letting you fall off the horse," he quickly added.

"Oh, that." *So much for moonlight and romance.* Her disappointment was so keen that her next words came out sounding sharper than usual.

"Look, you and I both know I made a fool of myself. I don't want to rehash the whole thing. All I really want is some peace and quiet."

"You haven't had much of that, have you?" To her surprise, his voice was filled with regret. "I'm sorry your visit didn't turn out the way you'd hoped, Dinosaur Lady."

She tried to study his face, but was unable to see it clearly in the failing light.

"What are you going to do if you don't find anything?" he asked quietly.

Noelle shrugged, and leaned forward against the fence railing again. She watched the mare crop at a few blades of grass. "Do my shows. Do my busywork over at CMP. The usual, I guess."

"You could always come back here on your weekends and days off."

"You'd actually let me keep searching?"

"Why not?"

Her gaze remained on the herd. "Because I can't help you if you're after more money."

"Money?"

"You heard me. We won't be able to make another deal. I might as well be honest, Matt. I've only been able to get enough pledges to cover the annual expenses for five patients. I doubt if I could get anyone else right now."

"Five patients? For a year?"

"Yes. I know it's not much... I wish it could be more, but we're just a small educational station. I'm afraid I won't be able to find you any more sponsors, at least not until next year's pledge drive."

There was a sudden silence, then Matt said, "First of all, having the annual expenses paid for five patients is more than I'd hoped for. Even one child is a miracle. Don't belittle your efforts. I certainly don't."

Noelle exhaled with relief, an emotion that disappeared as he added fiercely, "And I'm not talking about charging you admission to come back here."

Noelle jumped, his sudden vehemence startling her. "But I thought that's what this was all about. Money!"

"You thought wrong! Hell, and you think *I* twist words around."

To her amazement, he actually sounded insulted. That, and something else she couldn't quite define. . . .

"I want you to have free run of the ranch," he was saying. "You can keep looking here all you want. I don't care if you work straight through fall until the ground freezes and winter sets in."

"But—what about your patients?"

"I'll worry about my patients! You just worry about finding fossils."

Noelle couldn't believe what she was hearing. For a moment, she actually wondered if his offer revealed a personal interest—and the possibility thrilled her. No matter how she tried to deny it, Matt was beginning to carve a place in her life that she couldn't just dismiss. But her cautious side, the side of her that had been disappointed so many times, emerged.

"Why the sudden change of heart?"

"Because..." Matt hesitated. "Because of Jason."

She should have known it would be Jason on his mind. Not her.

"Jason," she repeated dully. She fought her disappointment and went back to watching the horses.

"Yes. You started something here, Noelle—something Jason needs to see finished. We all do. If there aren't any fossils, we need to know. If there are, we need to know that, too."

He reached for her chin and slowly turned her head his way. "We can't go on with this uncertainty hanging over us."

Noelle deliberately backed away from his touch. "And just who is 'we,' Matt?"

"You. Me. My riders. And Jason, of course."

Noelle steeled herself for the next question. "What about Alex?"

"Alex has nothing to do with it. This fossil business is between us," Matt said tersely.

"You're wrong! What happens if I find a rich fossil bed? How's Alex going to handle it all?"

"You let me worry about Alex. I've been taking care of him for a long time now."

"Maybe that's been Alex's problem all along," she said seriously. "Maybe Alex should take care of himself." Despite Matt's indrawn breath, she continued. "Matt, I know it's none of my business. I also know how you felt when I tried to suggest this before. But you're so busy championing the cause of the underdog, you can't see clearly! You're busy with Alex. Then there's your patients and your ranch. And let's not forget your lobby work."

His hands dropped from her arms. "What are you trying to say?"

"I'm saying that your life is not your own! What happened between you and Connie is a prime example."

"I don't know what you've heard about Connie, but she and I weren't right for each other. It only took a few movies and dinner dates to learn that. Alex had nothing to do with our decision to stop seeing each other."

"But what if you *had* been right for each other? You could have lost something very valuable if you'd let Alex influence you. Matt, try letting people fight their own battles sometimes! Concentrate on your own life. It would be better for you, and better for them. Especially Alex. Just step back for a change."

"Why? So I can watch my brother beat his head against the wall? So I can watch him turn into a cynic who expects nothing from life or the people around him?"

"He's like that already!"

"I'm sure an expert like you would know," he flung out.

Noelle gasped. "Is that what you think of me?" she asked hoarsely.

"What else can I think? It's the only part of yourself you've ever bothered to show me. The professional. The woman who's got an answer for everything. That's just a performance, Noelle—like being the Dinosaur Lady. You've hidden yourself away like your precious fossils. It's nice and safe in the museum, isn't it? And in the studio? Not like the real world."

Noelle gave him a tight smile. "You think Alex is living in the real world? Are you *letting* him?"

This time when she stepped away and hurried to the house, he didn't call her back.

Nor did he bring up the subject again in the days that followed.

Not even when her remaining search time was down to the last day. Matt had arranged for a farewell party; he'd invited the Swansons for an old-fashioned outdoor barbecue and they'd eagerly accepted.

Noelle wasn't looking forward to the festivities, but they'd been planned too far in advance to cancel. She'd decided to grit her teeth and make the best of it, which wasn't going to be easy. Both Alex and Matt were cool and distant. It appeared the Caldwell men had closed ranks against her. Jason himself was miserable about leaving Noelle to go back with the Swansons.

"Jason, please behave yourself!" Noelle whispered at the picnic table just as they'd all sat down. Jason had dropped ice down the back of one foster sister, splattered the shirt of another with the catsup squirt bottle, and was now busy shooting watermelon seeds at Alex with his fingers. "You know better!"

A surly Jason had ignored her. "I don't want to go home with *them*. They're not my real parents. And they have another foster kid coming. They won't have time for me."

"Sweetheart, I know you feel bad, but you can't stay here forever."

"Can't I go home with you?" Jason begged. "I promise I'll be good! I'll eat anything you fix, and do all my chores without being told, and I'll be really, really quiet when you're working."

"Oh, Jason, I wish I could, but I'm not a registered foster parent. The courts wouldn't permit it."

At that, Jason's expression became morose again. He turned his back on her and resumed shooting watermelon seeds until Mr. Swanson threatened to send him away until he could "find some table manners."

The rest of the barbecue was a dismal failure. Matt was silent, Jason's mood was no better than Alex's, the Swanson girls were cranky from being teased, and Mr. and Mrs. Swanson were deeply embarrassed over Jason's behavior.

As for Noelle, real depression set in when Mr. Swanson asked about Jason's and her suitcases. She didn't want to leave any more than Jason did. True, Matt had offered earlier to let her continue searching for fossils, but he hadn't repeated the offer since they'd fought that evening at the paddock. And Noelle suspected she'd be missing both Matt and Jason more than she'd ever guessed possible.

She tried to improve her mood by reminding herself that tomorrow morning she'd be back at the studio. At least the children there believed in her. But at the moment that seemed small consolation. Jason wouldn't even look her in the eye, and Matt wasn't much better. She honestly didn't know which hurt more. She watched Mr. Swanson reprimand Jason again; this time he was sent away from the table. Jason was near tears, and so was she.

Matt took a seat next to her at the picnic table and said quietly, "I wish there was something I could do for Jason. Now that his grand adventure is over, he's miserable."

"Some grand adventure," Noelle said in a choked voice as the Swanson girls attacked their dessert. Everyone else was merely toying with theirs. "No fossils. Not even a petrified sliver."

Matt shook his head. "It's not the fossils he's upset at losing, Noelle. It's you. And you're going to miss him just as much, aren't you?"

Noelle remained silent.

"Have you ever thought about taking him in?" Matt asked in an undertone. "Permanently?"

"Oh, yes," Noelle admitted with a fierce hunger in her soul. "But Jason deserves the very best out of life. He rates a stable home and two great parents, not some second-rate paleontologist from a third-rate museum.'' She couldn't prevent the bitterness for pouring forth—bitterness about her failed dreams and thwarted ambitions.

Matt rose abruptly. Out of the corner of her eye she watched him speak to the Swansons. At their nods, he went over to Jason.

The boy was seated on the ground, his back against a tree.

"Get up and get mounted,'' Matt ordered. "You and I and Dr. Forrest are going to take one last look around the creek bed before you go home.''

Jason's face lit up. "Right now?''

"Right now. Unless you'd rather skip the ride and finish dessert with everyone else.''

"No way!'' Jason grabbed his crutches and scrambled to his feet in record time. Bypassing Matt, he instantly headed toward Noelle's side. "Thanks, Dinosaur Lady. This is even better than dessert.''

"I'm glad you think so, Jason, but this was—'' *Matt's idea,* she started to say, but Matt interrupted.

"A great idea of hers, wasn't it, son?''

Noelle stared at Matt in confusion. "But it's not—''

"That's Dr. Forrest for you, Jason,'' Matt smoothly inserted. "She never gives up.'' His expression clearly said, *Don't ruin this for him.* So Noelle didn't. Within minutes he and Jason had saddled their horses. Already Matt had Jason smiling and laughing as if the dismal farewell party had never occurred. Noelle was grateful, so grateful she wished there was something she could do for Matt in exchange. And then she thought of a way.

"Aren't you going to help me up?'' she asked.

Matt stared at her. "But I thought . . .''

"There you go, trying to think for me again,'' she said with a smile. "It'll be faster if we ride tandem, and I know you'll take good care of me. Right, Jason?''

Jason nodded.

"See? You're outvoted. Now please get me up behind you.''

Eventually he did. She was still nervous, but since Jason's confidence in Matt was restored, she didn't care. It was the only thing that mattered right now. Little boys needed heroes in their lives, too—not just heroines. Soon the three of them were riding beside the creek banks.

"Where to, Dinosaur Lady?" Jason asked.

Noelle thought carefully. "I want to head back to the section of the dried creek bed upstream from where you made your original find."

"But we've looked there a million times!" Jason argued. "Don't you want to try someplace new?"

From behind Matt, Noelle shook her head. "There's a few shallow loops around there that I gave only a cursory check."

Matt peered over his shoulder at her. "Why cursory?"

"Because the creek bed is much deeper. Why dig through shallower layers when deeper areas are already exposed? But since the exposed layers turned up empty, well... It's a long shot, I know, but I'd still like to check it out."

Matt nodded. "You know the way, Jason. Take us there."

Jason urged his pony to a quicker pace on the creek bed trail. Matt continued his slower walk.

"I'm going to miss that boy," Matt suddenly said.

"You'll still have him once a week for his riding lesson," she reminded him.

"It won't be the same. The house will seem awfully quiet without the two of you around."

Noelle wished she could see his face. "I should think you'd be glad," she ventured.

"Glad?"

"Sure. I mean, having company must be hard on a couple of bachelors. You won't have Jason chattering on and on about fossils. Or me arguing with you about them," she added ruefully.

"I don't know. It felt kind of nice to have the house filled with people again. It reminded me of when my parents were alive...." His voice trailed off on a strange note, then returned to normal. "I suppose I'll have to settle for those weekend visits when you and Jason come back to look for fossils."

"You really want me to come back?" she asked, taking pains to hide the hope and, yes, elation in her voice.

"Of course. I remember telling you I did."

"And I remember asking you why you suddenly decided to take the risk. I never did get a straight answer."

"Maybe I've just realized that it could take years of searching before you found anything."

That wasn't exactly what Noelle was hoping to hear, and her disappointment made her next words sound harsh. "So basically you're just humoring me?"

Her arms were still around his waist and she swore she'd felt his breath catch.

But his words were terse, unemotional. "Not exactly," he said. "As long as you're happy, Jason's happy. His welfare is very important to me."

Suddenly she couldn't stand it any longer. "Let me down," she said. "I want to walk."

And walk she did. She searched the upper banks of the creek bed and the old, dried-out loops that occasionally appeared alongside. But there was nothing.

"I thought for *sure* we'd find something, Dinosaur Lady," Jason said with disgust.

"Maybe next time, Jason. We should probably be getting back. We've checked all the old loops."

Jason's face fell, and Noelle's heart was wrenched. She was determined to buy Jason a few more minutes. "Not all of them. We still haven't checked one last place."

"Where?" Jason demanded with youthful impatience, even as Matt glanced at his watch.

"Are you sure? It's getting late, and the Swansons are waiting." He extended his hand and pulled her behind him again.

"Where you first took me riding and the horse threw me," she said, her arms now around his waist. "There was a little gully there."

"Noelle, you're just making it harder for Jason by delaying the inevitable," he said in a low voice. For a moment, she thought Matt was going to insist on returning. But then he reined his horse to the west.

"One last look, and that's it," he said more loudly.

"Thank you, Matt."

"Thanks, Matt," Jason echoed.

At Matt's urging, they hurried, not wanting to keep the Swansons waiting too long. Jason rode parallel to them on his little pony, riding as close to the two of them as he could. Once they reached the loop, however, they split up.

"You take the left side, Dr. Forrest. I'll take the right," Jason suggested.

"I think I'd like to walk," Noelle said. "Matt, could I get down again, please?"

He reached around behind him, his arm around her waist, and lifted her from behind him. She slid down the side of the horse until her feet touched the ground.

"Should I get off, too?" Jason asked. "I brought my crutches."

Noelle smiled. "No, sweetheart, you search from the horse. I'm just going to take a quick peek." She stepped down into the hardened earth of the old creek loop. "It doesn't look like there's much to see here, anyway," she said.

"We should have brought a shovel," Jason moaned.

"Maybe." Noelle kicked at the ground with her foot, but it wasn't a soft gravel base as the creek bed was. It was hard, packed earth. Only a puff of dust rose at the motion, settling on her sneakers and jeans.

Matt sat quietly astride his horse as Noelle walked the whole circumference of the old loop twice.

"Anything?" he asked when she stopped.

"Not a darn thing. But I couldn't go home without checking." She started to climb out of the waist-high depression, then slipped. The sides weren't as well packed as the bottom.

Matt began to dismount. "Let me give you a hand up."

"No, Matt, I'm fine," Noelle said. "I'll just grab this dead tree here."

Only it wasn't a tree. It was an old, dead piece of wood that had lost its anchoring roots years ago. When Noelle grasped at it for support, the whole thing pulled free of the crumbling sides. Jason yelled as she fell to the bottom, still clutching the deadwood. Matt flew off his horse and was at her side in seconds, but Noelle was already standing up and brushing off her jeans.

"I'm fine, guys," she said, feeling a little foolish.

Matt didn't release his hands from her arms. "Are you sure?"

"I'm okay," she insisted. She looked up and for the first time ever wasn't confused by the emotion on Matt's face. It was a tenderness she'd been hoping to see for a long time. And now that she finally, joyously had, she was speechless.

"Noelle?"

He was waiting for her to say something, anything. But Jason was there, his presence inhibiting. Still, she could move even closer in his arms as she said with a shaky smile, "I always seemed to get knocked off my feet here, Matt. I—"

She froze as she stared at the corner of the gully once hidden by the dead wood. Automatically she took note of a certain irregularity in the earth—a certain formation, a certain color, a certain *shape* that screamed at her paleontologist's soul. Every muscle in her body froze.

Could it be? Could she actually have found what she'd sought for so long!

"Noelle?"

But Noelle was already pivoting in Matt's embrace to get a better view, her hands stretching out to touch the unbelievable.

Oh, yes. Oh, yes!

Her hands tightened into triumphant fists, then she was pushing Matt away from her.

"Noelle? What is it?" he asked as she sank to her knees on the crumbling incline. "What's wrong?"

Her heart was pounding and she couldn't seem to catch her breath. *He doesn't see it! He doesn't understand!* But she couldn't stop to explain now.

Jason suddenly gasped aloud, fumbling for his crutches. "Matt, get me off this horse! Get me down!"

Noelle had waited a lifetime already! She refused to wait another second! With her bare hands, she frantically began to dig.

"I see you," she whispered hoarsely. "You're here, my prehistoric friend. I just know it."

She ignored broken nails, ignored Matt's questions, ignored everything except those few protruding inches above the soil.

Then her fingers froze into dirt-filled fists that hovered in the air. For a moment time stood still as she gazed upon the exposed, permineralized surface of fossilized bone—the graceful, tapering shape of unbroken jaw.

"Yes! Oh, yes, yes, yes…" she said over and over again. She closed her eyes in an exquisite moment of pure rapture, the protective soil sifting out of her fingers. She'd done it. She'd actually discovered a fossil! Noelle hugged herself with joy, then opened her eyes again to make sure she wasn't really dreaming. She saw Matt, his eyes as wide as hers as he stared at her find.

"Matt?" she whispered. "Do you see it? Jason, how about you? Isn't it beautiful?"

Jason smiled, the biggest smile she'd ever seen. Matt just stared, his gaze on the sharp, smooth, unmistakable piece of fossilized bone.

"Look at it! Matt, just look at it!"

Matt continued to gape, even as he went to rescue an excited Jason, who was ready to fall off the horse just to get to her. Jason ignored the crutches Matt was trying to hand him and practically launched himself off the side of the gully. Noelle caught him, braces and all, and his arms wrapped tightly around her neck. Jason was talking a mile a minute; she was laughing. She lifted Jason off his feet and spun him around and around in a joyous, triumphant dance.

"You did it! You did it!" Jason said, breathless, when Noelle finally stopped. "I knew you'd do it!"

"Oh, Jason, I'm so glad you were here to see this!" she gasped.

Jason buried his face in her shoulder and hugged her. She kissed his cheek, then the top of his head as she caught her breath. She couldn't believe her incredible good fortune. She wanted to share it with the world!

"Look at me, Matt!" She lifted a radiant face to him. "I'm a *real* Dinosaur Lady now!"

CHAPTER EIGHT

EVEN WHEN THE WILD JOY had subsided, the three of them stared at the jaw for the longest time. Matt joined them in the hole, bringing Jason his forgotten crutches after tying the pony. The setting sun threw long shadows over the three watchers as they stood there speechless. It was Noelle who finally broke the silence.

"This jaw..." Noelle's brain suddenly seemed to click, and she gasped. Her voice trembled with excitement. "I think I know what we have! This jaw is unique enough to identify it."

"Tell me!" Jason insisted, his fingers clamping down so hard on his crutches that Noelle wondered if she'd see dents in the aluminum.

"Yes, tell us," Matt seconded.

The Dinosaur Lady smiled at her audience and decided to play out the moment. "I'll have to uncover all of it before we can be certain, but let's see if Jason can make an educated guess. See how enormous the jaw structure is?"

"It's pretty big," Jason said.

"Look right here." She pointed with a dirty finger to the exposed hole sockets for teeth, and then back. "If I'm right, these are expandable jaws."

"Like a snake's?"

"Yes, and that's the clue here. That prey could be devoured in huge bites."

Jason bit his lip, unable to come up with an answer.

"It's a very rare dinosaur," Noelle hinted. "They've only discovered three so far. The last was found just a few years ago in our Morrison Formation—in Fort Collins, of course."

To any paleontologist, even an amateur one, the last clue was a dead giveaway. *"Epanterias!"* Jason shouted. "Is it an *Epanterias?"*

"Good for you, Jason! Matt, if I'm right, we're looking at only the fourth find ever made."

"I'm not familiar with the name. But I'm glad Jason was here to see it."

Despite her excitement, Noelle couldn't help but notice that Matt didn't include himself in that statement.

"Epanterias is the last evolved species of the *Allosaur* line," Jason proudly filled in. "They lived in North America 130 million years ago. They were meat-eaters, right, Dinosaur Lady? About the same size as the T-rex."

"Yes, and they've proven very, very difficult to find," Noelle added, refusing to let Matt's less-than-enthusiastic response take away from the moment. "The other three *Epanterias* discoveries were unearthed decades apart. A complete skeleton has never been discovered. That's why this find is so important—if I'm right, that is."

"You're never wrong, Dinosaur Lady. Wouldn't it be neat if we dug up a whole one? We'd both be famous." Jason sighed with bliss. "We'd be in the newspapers and everything."

"No newspapers," Matt said sharply. "No media at all, Jason."

"Oh, yeah. I forgot."

There was an embarrassed silence.

"This is silly. Just look at us," Noelle finally said, her arm still around Jason's shoulders. "We're standing here like we've just found a holy relic. We've got work to do."

"Matt? Are you going to help us?" Jason asked.

Matt remained silent. He stared at the fossil and even reached out toward it. Noelle caught at his hand. "Don't, Matt. Until we determine its condition, excessive handling is the worst thing for any find."

Matt withdrew his hand, and Noelle pushed the hair back from her face to cover the awkward moment.

"I'll need my tools and plaster and my camera. And I need to rope off the area, and—and—" She paused breathlessly, the sheer immensity of the task ahead overwhelming her.

"Calm down, Noelle. You know you can't do all that tonight. And Jason needs to get back to the stables. It's getting dark."

Trust Matt to be the voice of reason—at least when it comes to fossils. "He's right, Jason. We've got to wait until tomorrow."

Despite Jason's protests, she reluctantly covered the fossil with slow, careful stokes, knowing the soil would safeguard it, as it had for millions of years.

And with that, they left. The horses were stabled and the news was announced. The Swansons reacted with obvious pleasure. Alex didn't react at all. Ignoring both her and Matt, he mumbled something about checking on the horses and left. Noelle didn't have time to worry about it as the Swansons unsuccessfully tried to get an overexcited Jason in the car. It wasn't until she spoke to him that he finally behaved.

"Remember what I told you," she said, hugging him. "Good paleontologists need to learn to follow directions. And you need your rest if you want to be my assistant. So you listen to your foster parents, okay?"

Jason promised, and Mrs. Swanson gave Noelle a grateful look. Then they were off, leaving just Noelle and Matt, and the stillness of the Colorado night. Finally all the excitement of the discovery seemed to catch up with her. She just had to sit down. Noelle collapsed on the bench of the now-cleared picnic table. In the distance, a mare softly nickered to her filly, then silence reigned.

"Congratulations," Matt said. He joined her, but on the opposite side of the table. "Your hunch paid off."

"Thank you. I still can't believe it. I can't believe you suggested it, either."

Matt shook his head at the irony of it all. "And on the last day of your search, too."

"I'm so very glad you did, Matt. And I'm glad you let Jason come with me. I don't know which of us was more excited...." Noelle sighed contentedly.

"He was pretty thrilled."

"Yes." Noelle tilted her head and studied him. "But you weren't."

Silence. "I suppose shocked is more like it."

"You never expected me to find anything, did you?"

"No, I guess I didn't. But I should have known that if anyone could, it would be you. So, Dinosaur Lady, what happens next?"

"I think," she said slowly, "that it's time for a new deal, don't you?"

"Always the career women," Matt said with a wry twist of his lips.

"And why not?" Noelle said, defending herself. "Our last deal might have had a few rough edges, but it all worked out. You have all my pledge contacts and paperwork in your office. I have my fossil find, with promises of more to come, and your patients haven't suffered. And Jason's in paleontologist's paradise."

"Yes. Even my brother has managed to survive."

Noelle shivered in the dark, telling herself it was the evening air and not Alex's name that caused the chills down her spine.

"I must admit, Noelle, everything did work out. So if you're up to a new deal, I'm game."

"I'm up to anything, as long as I get to have any future fossils. You haven't changed your mind about that, have you?"

"No. I sure as hell don't want it, nor any others you may find."

Noelle exhaled a sigh of relief, a sigh that was cut short as he added, "But with the same restrictions. No press, no publicity, no museums."

"Agreed."

"Unfortunately, we have a problem here."

"Problem?" she echoed. The hairs on the back of her neck prickled a warning. "What *kind* of problem?"

"You can't dig right now."

"Are you *serious?*" She couldn't believe her ears. "I've waited all my life for this!"

Matt reached for her hand. "Let's go back to the house. We can talk inside."

"We can talk here." Noelle deliberately avoided his grasp. There was no way she was getting her suitcases and leaving until this was settled.

"There can't be a dig yet, Dinosaur Lady." Matt's voice was firm. "I know how much this means to you, but—"

"*Do you?* Do you really?"

"Yes. But you can't go tearing up the creek bed and its sides right now. It's my major trail for the less-experienced riders, because of the high walls and deep gravel. Remember what I told you about my mounts when we first met?"

Noelle nodded, her throat tight. "They have to be kept to a strict routine."

"Yes. I can't disrupt that routine so suddenly. I'll have to gradually retrain the horses—and riders—before you do any excavating."

"How long would that take? A few weeks?"

"More like a few months."

Her jaw dropped at the news.

"A few months! Matt, it's August already! By the time the horses are retrained the ground will be hard, even frozen. I can't dig in the winter."

"I realize that, and I'm sorry. Still, you have to understand. The horses could learn quickly enough, but the same can't be said for all my patients. Many have slow learning abilities and poor retention. I can't put their safety at risk."

"I could stay on the banks," Noelle said quickly. "I'd leave the bed alone. Your beginner's trail would be quite safe."

Matt shook his head. "Jason's find was in the creek bed, and yours was on the bank. Noelle, I'm not a paleontologist, but I know enough to guess you'll draw a line between the two and excavate anything in between."

"I wouldn't touch the bed, Matt."

"Even if you didn't...all that extra activity up on the banks would be a major distraction to both horses and riders." He shook his head. "I can't chance it. You'll have to wait until the spring."

Noelle took one look at Matt's face and knew she wouldn't win this argument. She nodded reluctantly. "With the exception of the fossil we found today."

"The jaw?"

"Yes. It's already accessible. In fact, it's exposed enough to be damaged by the winter. I remove only the jaw, then come back in the spring."

Matt's gaze was piercing. "And just how long would this removal take?"

"Not long. I'm guessing a week. If it's anchored in solid rock and I have to chisel it free, a couple of weeks at the most. I could work after hours so as not to disturb any riders."

There was a long silence. Then Matt rose. He leaned on the table and studied her sharply.

"What if there's a motherlode of dead dinosaurs behind that jaw? Do you honestly think you could quit at just one fossil?"

Noelle stood, too, and met his gaze head on. "You'd be surprised what I can do when the stakes are high. I remove the single fossil piece that's exposed. Then I stop. Period."

"And you won't say anything to anyone? Not the museum, not the studio, not even your family?" His voice was deadly serious. "I can't have people with fossil fever running wild on my ranch, especially while I'm retraining the horses and riders. If you want full rights to any fossils here, there will be *no* digging until I say so. Understand?"

"You have my word. I'll keep it."

"See that you do."

"Don't worry, Matt." She held out her hand for him to shake. "Everything worked out before. It'll work out this time, too." *I hope...*

"YOU HAVEN'T BEEN yourself since you left that dude ranch," Louise remarked as she put blusher on Noelle's cheeks. "Is something wrong, Dr. Forrest?"

Noelle sighed. Yes, something was wrong, all right. She had everything she'd ever wanted in her career right at her fingertips, yet was forbidden to speak of it. Matt's reasons were valid, of course; Noelle realized that.

But she felt heartsick. Her first waking thought was of the fossil site on Matt's ranch. Her last despairing thought at night was the number of days until next spring, the months and months before she could arrange a full dig and discover if there were more fossils. And in between those waking and sleeping hours, visions of the anchored jaw nagged at her.

The exposed portion of the fossil was three-quarters free, but the rest was stubbornly encased in a slab of hard sandstone. Despite its name, sandstone had to be chipped away sliver by agonizing sliver, and she had to do it during what little free time she had.

Thanks to her three-week "vacation" at Matt's ranch, she was not only behind with her work at the studio, she was way behind at CMP. Locating a free block of time was almost as frustrating as chipping away at the slab of rock holding her treasure. To make things worse, she had fossil fever, and she had it *bad*. She knew it was unhealthy—knew it was even obsessive—but for the life of her, Noelle couldn't get that fossilized jaw out of her mind.

She'd had her worst fight with Matt over it. As often as she could, she drove out to his ranch. She never had much time to work before dark, and one evening, when she would have rushed away to the dig site, he grabbed her arm and stopped her.

"Would you quit mooning over that damn fossil for just one minute and listen to me?"

"What is it?" she asked, glancing at the tools still in her truck. "You aren't having second thoughts, are you? I haven't mentioned the find to anyone except you and Jason. I've kept my part of the deal."

"And stop talking about our deal! I'm sick to death of that word!"

"Then what do you want?" she asked impatiently, knowing sunset wasn't long off. "What's wrong?"

"Jason is what's wrong! He asks about you—talks about you—all the time! But you never see him. Have you dumped the boy now that you've hit the big time?"

Finally Matt had her whole, undivided attention.

"Of course not! I'll have you know I talk to Jason almost every night on the phone!"

"Then why isn't he here with you?" Matt demanded.

"Because I'm working two jobs and trying to play catchup at both of them! Because my schedule's a mess, and no one's cutting me any slack because I can't tell them about my find! The few times I *have* been free, Jason hasn't, or he's back in class now that school's started again. I've checked. I've even been over to his house."

"I heard about that, too." Matt crossed his arms across his chest. "The Swansons say you've totally disrupted Jason's life. He's become difficult and hard to live with. Maybe I was wrong before. Cutting him out of your life might be a kindness in the long run."

"That's not true! A child's entitled to have friends, and I'm not giving Jason up unless it's *his* idea, not yours. And as for the Swansons..."

Her eyes had sparked with fury. "Maybe they're overextended. Maybe if they spent *more* time with Jason and *less* time worrying about taking in another foster child, he wouldn't be so miserable. It's bad enough that he always comes second to the Swansons' adopted children. Now he has to do the same to some other child he hasn't even seen yet! The Swansons have the best intentions in the world, but they're trying to do too much—and Jason's paying the price."

Matt hesitated. "You may have a point there," he conceded, "but debating the flaws of this state's foster care system isn't going to help. You've made Jason a part of your life, and now suddenly you're not there for him anymore. What do you intend to do about it? Or *are* you going to do anything about it?"

Stung, Noelle had retaliated with an attack of her own. "Why don't you worry about *yourself*, Mr. High and Mighty? Jason idolizes you. He talked about you and his riding the very first time I met him. He also told me that every time he tries to get close to you, Alex pushes him away. No matter that Jason is a child with no family at all. No matter that Alex is so possessive he can't stand Jason's presence. No matter that Jason was in tears when he told me the whole story."

"Jason was crying?" Matt's voice was suddenly hoarse.

"Because of Alex. Jason was afraid Alex would inhibit our friendship. But unlike you, I told Jason I wouldn't let Alex interfere."

He'd stared at her, his expression shocked, but for once Noelle hadn't cared.

"You want to start passing out blame where Jason's unhappiness is concerned?" she'd asked. "Why don't you start with yourself?"

Matt blanched under his tan, and Noelle took the opportunity to shake free of his grip. "Now, let me go. I have work to do."

That had been a week ago. Matt hadn't waited for her arrivals anymore, nor had he tried to contact her. More than once she'd picked up the phone to call him, but what could she say? She desperately wanted to see Matt, talk to him. She daydreamed about being held, being kissed by him. But she couldn't apologize for telling the truth any more than she could help wanting to get her hands on that fossil.

Noelle was miserable.

And now even her makeup artist had noticed it.

"Well, Louise, I guess you could say I have man troubles." That was certainly a fact. Jason and Matt were both driving her crazy.

"Oh, no," Louise groaned with real dismay. "Who's the guy this time?"

"Guys. As in plural. I'm at my wits' end."

"You're seeing two guys at once?"

"You could say that."

"But you never have before.... I mean, isn't that a bit, well, confusing?" Louise tactfully asked.

"You don't know the half of it." But how could she explain it all to Louise, when she couldn't even explain it to herself?

Things had been a mess ever since she'd located the fossil. Matt was clearly unhappy, and Jason was more despondent than she'd ever known him, despite her continued daily phone calls. She'd even managed to take him out to the dig site a few times.

The only good that had come out of this was Matt's spending more time with Jason. Unfortunately, it didn't seem to be enough. All her conversations with the boy ended with him pleading to see her again. She always hung up wishing she could make things better for him, yet not knowing how. And now the turmoil of her personal life was spilling into her professional life.

Her performance on *Fun with Fossils* had become lacklustre, and ratings had started to slip. She had to snap out of it.

"Five minutes, Dinosaur Lady," a staff member yelled out.

Noelle nodded her acknowledgement. As she shrugged into her blazer and adjusted her portable mike, she compared today's artificial stage persona to the vitally alive woman digging on Matt's creek bank. Or was she really comparing a life with Matt and Jason to a life without them?

It wasn't fair, she thought as she stepped out onto the set amid cheering children. Everything she'd ever wanted was now within her reach.

Then why did she feel so bad?

CHAPTER NINE

"ARE WE REALLY CHISELING the rest of the fossil out to-day?" Jason asked eagerly.

The two of them were fossil hunting together again; on this particular Saturday, their schedules had finally meshed. Noelle had called an excited Jason early that morning, then picked him up right after his lunch. It was now late afternoon, and although they were dirty, grimy and hot from the September sun, their spirits still ran high.

"We most certainly are. A few more inches of rock and we'll have the whole thing free. In fact, I'll even let you pull it out while I take pictures."

"Oh!" Jason's eyes grew round as silver dollars, his fists tightly clenching his chisel and mallet. "Could I?"

"Yep. I'll certainly be needing those strong muscles of yours," Noelle replied.

Jason lifted one arm and flexed it. "I'm ready when you are." Then he stopped posing and inched closer to the work area. "Hurry up, Dinosaur Lady!" he urged. "Oh, I hope there's another fossil behind this one. And I hope it's a big one."

Noelle laughed aloud. As far as Jason was concerned, the bigger the fossil, the better. It wasn't exactly the most scientific of assumptions, but she didn't have the heart to correct him. She adjusted her safety goggles in preparation to start chiseling again just as Matt rode up.

"Hi, Matt," Jason sang out. "We're almost done freeing the fossil. Wanna watch?"

"Sounds good to me," Matt replied. He dismounted, tied his horse and approached the edge of the depression. "Hello, Noelle."

"Hello, Matt." She kept her eyes on her work and promised herself that this time, she and Matt would manage to be civil. Maybe even friendly... Or more?

"A couple of swings here," she said, "and—finally! It's actually free! I can feel it." She pushed the goggles to the top of her head just as Jason reached for the fossil to pull it out.

"Jason, wait!" Matt interrupted. "Noelle should be the one to remove the fossil." Jason's face fell even as Noelle said, "No, Matt, it's okay. I told him he could do it."

"I thought you'd want the honors."

"That's not important to me," she said evenly. "But I need to get my camera so we can document this." She retrieved it from her backpack. "Okay, sweetheart, I'm ready. Go ahead."

Jason needed no further encouragement. Noelle gave Jason a thumbs-up, then focused her camera.

"Easy, Jason," Noelle reminded, her finger on the shutter button. "Take your time, and don't drop it. There's some rock, but most of it's bone, and we don't want to damage it. Just gently slide the fossil onto the tarp."

"I know, Dinosaur Lady," Jason said with all the confidence of youth. With careful, lifting motions, he freed the fossil from the dirt. But instead of sliding it onto the tarp lying right beneath the hole, he cradled the fossil gently, almost reverently, in his lap.

"Just look at it," Jason whispered.

Noelle captured his rapt enchantment on film, then, unable to stand by any longer, passed the camera to Matt. "Move over, Jason, and let me see."

By the end of another hour, much of the rough dirt and debris from the jaw lay on the tarp, thanks to Noelle's and Jason's brushes, whisks and probes. Their progress was all documented on film by Matt.

"Do you still think it's an *Epanterias*?" Jason asked.

"Yes, I do."

"Do you think my fossil could be part of one?"

"I can't say, Jason. Yours was weathered so much from lying out in the open, it couldn't tell us much. But almost half of this one is encased in sandstone. The rock and soil kept it in much better condition. Watch, I'll show you the difference. This sandstone section here should break away in one large chunk. I've just about got it loose. A few more taps—"

Suddenly the whole side slab loosened. Jason went to grab it, but Noelle was faster. She caught it in her free hand and carefully pulled it away from the main body.

A row of hidden fossil teeth was finally exposed.

Matt reached for the camera and took another shot.

"It's beautiful," Jason whispered in an awe-struck voice.

"I wish I could tell if we had the whole thing. It'll be easier to see once the anchoring bed of stone is removed. But that will take time."

Noelle laid the fossil on a waiting burlap tarp, pulled a whisk brush from her back pocket and gently dusted away some soil on the newly exposed teeth. "For now this is good enough. More than good enough."

She watched Matt study the fossil. Half of it was recognizable bone. The rest disappeared into sandstone. "How long will it take you to chip all this rock off?"

"A few inches a day," Jason quickly replied.

"That long?"

"Unless there are other fractures that will break off like this one did, yes. It's slow work, but I don't mind it. We're lucky to have found this rock chunk in one piece."

Jason nodded. "Usually sandstone this narrow splinters and breaks. This jaw could have splintered with it. We were lucky." Jason then stared into the hole left by the removed fossil and frowned. "I can't see anything else in here."

Noelle had to smile. "We can't make a find every day, Jason. We have to deal with first things first. Like wrapping this piece in burlap and covering it with plaster."

"I'll do it!" Jason volunteered.

"That's the least of your worries. How are you getting this fossil back to your car?" Matt asked. "Even if I had a set of saddlebags with me, it's far too large to fit."

"I don't know if I'd want it bouncing around on a horse, anyway," Noelle said uneasily.

"How about if Jason and I ride back and return with my Jeep?" Matt asked.

Noelle glanced at her watch. "No, that'll take too long, and I promised Mrs. Swanson I'd get Jason home in time for dinner. Jason, don't argue," she said as Jason opened his mouth. "She was very strict in her instructions."

"I can always get the fossil for you tomorrow," Matt volunteered.

Both Noelle and Jason stared at him.

"Are you crazy?" Jason actually said.

"Jason, mind your manners," Noelle said gently. "It was just a suggestion."

"Obviously not a very good one," Matt responded.

"I'll walk it out," Noelle decided. She started emptying out her oversize backpack. "I'd rather come back for my tools and things later."

"I was afraid you'd say that," Matt remarked as he dismounted. "How long will it take that stuff to dry?"

"The plaster? Not long at all. See?"

Noelle gestured toward Jason. He had finished mixing the premeasured packets of plaster with canteen water and was already applying it to the burlap.

"It's professionally made to be quick-setting." Noelle watched his progress, but could find nothing to correct in Jason's actions.

"Good. As soon as it dries, load up the fossil, then give me your pack. I'll carry it back for you."

Noelle hesitated. "Matt, it's a good-sized chunk of rock!"

Matt's response was to take the pack from her arms. "I don't mind a little inconvenience in the name of science. Unless Jason's afraid I'll drop it."

"Nope. Matt's never dropped a patient yet. He'll take good care of it, Dinosaur Lady."

"Thanks for the vote of confidence, son." Matt gave Jason a friendly clap on the shoulder. "Now, if we can just convince the Dinosaur Lady here."

Noelle watched the two of them together, happy to see no strain between them. She felt even happier that there was no longer any strain between her and Matt.

"If you really don't mind, then, thank you."

"Don't thank me yet." He grinned. "You get to ride the horse all the way back without any help from me."

Noelle's protests were drowned out by the sound of Jason's laughter. "He's just teasing, Dinosaur Lady. I'll lead Matt's horse."

"Jason's right."

"Trust you both to give me a hard time," she said, but there was no sting in her words. While they waited for the plaster to set, she carefully took a few final documenting photographs, then secured a tarp over both her tools and the dig area. Then, when Matt wasn't looking, she quickly snapped a photo of him.

His arm was around Jason's shoulders, and the two of them were deep in conversation. She wanted something to remember this day by. She took one more picture, then slung the camera around her neck. The last thing she did before loading the fossil on Matt's back was to set red warning flags around the shallow hole.

"Ready now?" he asked as he adjusted the straps of her pack.

She nodded.

"Then let's go."

Despite the rather unorthodox method of travel, the fossil made it safely to Noelle's car. The two horses were now back in the stable. Jason had been retrieved by the Swansons, who'd been waiting when he rode back with Matt. But he said goodbye to Noelle and eventually left without complaining.

The sun was hovering just above the western peaks of the Rocky Mountains by the time Noelle and Matt reached the main ranch complex. Matt walked her to her car.

"I hope it won't be too difficult to work on the fossil at home," he said.

"That's not a problem." For once she wouldn't have to compete with the senior staff at the museum. The fossil would be all hers. "Thanks for carrying it back for me, Matt. I really appreciate this." She paused. "I guess this is goodbye until next spring?"

"It's not goodbye yet," Matt said casually. "You still have to come back to get your tools."

Noelle bit her lip. "I wish I had them now. I can't work on the fossil without them." Was it her imagination, or did Matt actually look disappointed at her response?

"We can take the Jeep out there now and save you a trip tomorrow, if that's what you want."

"I..." It wasn't what she wanted, not really. She did have her career to think about. Somehow, though, she couldn't work up the old enthusiasm. Even the thought of the fossilized jaw locked in her car trunk, exciting as that was, didn't make her feel any better about leaving. In a very real way, the ranch had begun to feel like home. "I...suppose I really should finish my business."

"Fine," Matt said stiffly. "I'll run inside for my keys, and we'll get your tools."

Noelle mustered her courage. "I hope we can keep in touch."

"On a professional basis, you mean," was the curt response.

Noelle took in a deep breath. "No, on a personal basis. That is, if you want..."

Matt's welcome smile was the answer she'd hoped for. And the quick, brushing kiss he gave her lips was a happy bonus.

A few minutes later they were on the dirt trails, the Jeep's headlights peering through the evening dimness. Noelle grabbed onto the roll bar as Matt drove over a particularly bumpy patch of ground.

"We're almost at the creek bed, Noelle. Hold on."

In a few minutes the Jeep's headlights illuminated the dig site.

It seemed to Noelle that Matt was out of the vehicle before it even stopped. She followed more slowly. Not until she heard his muffled oath did she make any real effort to hurry.

"Oh, no!" She couldn't believe her eyes. The red flags had been uprooted, their wooden stakes snapped in half. The tarp had been ripped away from the opening, then slashed, shredded and scattered. And the soil she'd carefully layered over the exposed hole and sandstone base of the jaw had been rudely pushed aside. As for her tools...

Noelle sank to her knees. The delicate picks, probes and smaller chisels had been smashed or destroyed. And all the dead wood, rocks and weeds she and Jason had so painstakingly cleared out had been thrown over what was left of her tools.

Matt knelt by her side. They silently took in the surrounding chaos. It was Matt who spoke first.

"I don't know what happened here."

"I don't, either...." Noelle's voice shook as she stared at the destruction before her. It was so calculated, so malicious. Dear lord, if she hadn't insisted on removing the fossilized jaw, it could have been among the carnage.... Thank heavens it was safely locked away in her trunk.

"I have a flashlight in my Jeep. What can I do to help?"

"I don't think there's much we can do except clean up the mess."

"Noelle, I'm sorry."

She drew in a deep breath. "It's okay. The fossil's safe."

"Who could have done this?"

"I—" Noelle froze. There was only one person who would have dared to do this, only one man who had the motive and the opportunity. But did she risk telling Matt the truth?

"Go on, Noelle. I'm listening." His voice was so filled with concern, that suddenly she felt she could.

She sank onto the dirt and rested her soiled hands on her knees. "I wonder where your brother was this evening."

"Alex?" The name exploded sharply from Matt's lips. "You think Alex did this?"

"I think you should ask him," Noelle said quietly. "Alex doesn't believe in my work. He never has."

There was a long, terrible silence that seemed to drag on and on. Finally Matt rose to his feet. The headlights of the

Jeep revealed the harsh planes of his face. Without a word he retrieved some of the broken flags and a section of tarp that was still serviceable.

"Get what's left of your tools," Matt said in a tight voice. "Let's secure this area for the night."

With a heavy heart, she did. It didn't take long. There wasn't much they could salvage.

"Let's get back to the house," he said.

The two of them made their way to the Jeep in a miserable silence that continued all the way back to the house. When Matt finally shut off the engine, Noelle opened her own door, then hesitated.

"Do you want me to go with you or should I just leave?" she asked.

"I think my brother has the right to hear what you've said in person."

"You—you do believe me, don't you, Matt?"

Matt said nothing. He simply reached for her arm, and led her first to the office, where she washed her hands and retrieved her purse. Then they headed for the living room. Alex was alone and watching a comedy on television. Matt grabbed the remote control and shut off the program. He tossed it on the coffee table and remained standing, with Noelle at his side.

"Noelle and I just came back from the dig site again. Someone has vandalized it."

"I did," Alex replied without a moment's hesitation. "It took me a while to find a chance to follow you out there, or I would have done it much sooner."

Noelle swayed on her feet. Never in a million years would she have thought Alex would confess. It was almost as if he wanted her to suffer.

Matt and Noelle spoke at the same moment. "You admit it?" "Alex, how *could* you?"

Alex addressed Matt, pointedly ignoring Noelle. "She's no good for us, Matt. Not for us, or for the ranch. We both knew that from the first. I waited for you to get rid of her, but it appears Dr. Forrest's charms were too much for you.

So I did what you should have done the moment Jason babbled about your precious fossil site.''

"Are you proud of yourself, Alex? Are you proud of your carefully planned destruction?" Noelle asked.

"I wanted to make sure you got the message." His eyes bored right into hers. "I thought if I destroyed your fossil, you'd leave."

Noelle felt grateful again that she'd already locked the fossil in her car trunk, away from Alex's destructive hands.

"Matt has a responsibility to the other patients here," he was saying. "Unfortunately, my brother went out of his way to help *you*. I never thought I'd see Matt play pack mule to a piece of rock and bone. It's pathetic. It shows just how dangerous a woman you are."

"You were watching us?" Matt demanded.

Alex nodded and finally acknowledged Noelle's presence with a smile, but a smile that made Noelle shiver. The hostility that had always disturbed her was back in full force. Just the thought of his stalking her was chilling.

"Your charms—and your luck—must be considerable, Dr. Forrest. But I see right through you. I always have."

At the unnerving glitter in his eyes, Noelle took an involuntary step backward.

"Either way, the end result is the same. I'm guessing you won't stick around here for long."

Alex reached for the remote and turned the television back on. "Now if you don't mind, I'd really like to see the end of this show."

Matt's expression was unreadable as he turned toward Noelle. "I need to speak to my brother in private."

"You want me to leave? But how can I? This concerns me, too! What about the dig site? How are you going to keep it safe? And my tools? They cost hundreds of dollars, Matt!"

Silence. There had been too many silences between her and Matt. Suddenly, the painful truth struck home. Alex hadn't forced Noelle's hand as he'd planned. She'd escaped with the fossil intact. But Alex had certainly forced Matt's. Matt would be forced to choose between her—an outsider—and his brother. Noelle didn't need a crystal ball to guess what the outcome would be.

That thought was terrifying.

"I'll cover the cost of your tools, Noelle," Matt was saying. "Just send me the bill."

Noelle gasped. "You're going to let him get away with this?"

"What would you have me do, Noelle? Set up an armed guard? Or call the police and have my brother arrested?"

"Maybe that wouldn't be such a bad idea," Noelle whispered. "He needs to be held responsible for his actions. He's a grown man, Matt. You have to stop protecting him."

"He's my brother!"

Noelle looked from Matt to Alex, then back to Matt again. "You'd never allow this from one of your patients."

"Alex is more than just a patient. He's family." Matt's voice was icy.

"And Alex takes full advantage of that! Matt, can't you see? By not making him accountable, you're crippling Alex far worse than any airplane crash ever could!"

There was a deathly quiet in the room, despite the sound from the television. Alex's face was a terrible white. But the expression in Matt's eyes frightened her even more than Alex's.

"I think you'd better go."

Noelle hardly recognized the voice as Matt's, but his expression brooked no refusal. And with her heart in her throat, Noelle left, with the sounds of Alex's television show following her out into the darkness.

Noelle was never able to remember how she managed to get herself home that night. She must have been on autopilot; her mind certainly wasn't on her driving. For the first time in her life, she had to face the fact that she was desperately, irrevocably in love. The agony she was experiencing at Matt's rejection of her was proof enough of that.

Not that she needed any proof. She'd been drawn to Matt Caldwell from the very first. His compassion for his family and patients coupled with his awareness of her was a hard combination to resist. And despite his reservations he'd gone out of his way to help her. And Jason.

Unfortunately, all that meant little without loyalty. And— right or wrong—Matt's first loyalty was to his family. It was as simple as that.

The realization was devastating. So devastating, in fact, that Denver's Dinosaur Lady left her precious find untouched on her workbench that night, turned off the light and prayed that, come morning, Matt Caldwell would have a change of heart.

That was not to be. As day after anxious day went by, Noelle slowly began to lose hope. Except for a few inches she'd halfheartedly chipped away, the fossil still remained encased in its sandstone tomb. Noelle spent more time willing the phone to ring than working on the retrieved fossil. Finally she abandoned work on the jawbone altogether until she could concentrate enough to complete the delicate task.

The phone did ring one day, but the person calling was never the one Noelle wanted to hear. The studio called once to confirm her taping sessions, and Jason Reilly called to set up their next dig date. "I'm afraid you're not going to be doing any digging for a while," Noelle told him.

"Why not?" Jason asked anxiously. "Can't I still be your assistant?"

"Of course you can, Jason," Noelle replied, searching wildly for an excuse to give him. She didn't want to tell Jason that because of Alex and because of Matt's patients, Matt wouldn't let her dig at the site until next spring. But she didn't want to lie to Jason, either.

"I've decided to work on cleaning up the jaw before we dig anymore."

"Can I help?"

Noelle smiled. Jason was the one beam of sunshine in this whole mess. "As long as you keep up your grades in school. I'll talk to Mrs. Swanson as soon as I get my schedule from the studio."

Jason had to be satisfied with that. Noelle could only pray that Jason wouldn't ask Matt too many questions during his next riding lesson. After last night, she didn't think the subject of fossils—or the Dinosaur Lady—would be Matt's favorite topic of discussion with Jason.

Or with anyone, Noelle thought dismally. She decided to take matters into her own hands and tried to call Matt at his office, but was only able to reach the receptionist.

"I can't promise he'll return your call," was the apologetic reply, "but I'll give him the message."

After that, there was nothing left to do but turn on the answering machine and head downtown for the studio and her afternoon taping of *Fun with Fossils*.

As always, her studio was filled with excited children all eager to see the Dinosaur Lady. Noelle presented her material with an enthusiasm she was far from feeling. Her talk on the creation of the famous Morrison Formation was the same talk she'd given Matt, which didn't help her despondent mood. Nonetheless, she felt she owed everyone more than just a cursory delivery of the facts.

The show went well. By the time the taping was over, the audience was enthralled. As affectionate young fans gathered around her for autographs, Noelle was able to congratulate herself. She'd been able to put aside her personal feelings and give her viewers the kind of program they deserved.

She even managed to maintain her composure on the drive home—until she reached the parking lot for her third-floor apartment and saw Matt's Jeep. As she climbed out of her own car, her welcoming smile faded. Matt wasn't inside. Alex was.

Noelle looked into his wild eyes. Something was terribly wrong. "Alex? What is it? Is Matt all right?"

"There's nothing wrong with my brother, and you damn well know it." Alex's voice dripped scorn. "Don't pretend you don't know what you've done!"

"Done? What have I done?"

"Let's talk inside," Alex said. "And don't look at me like that. Cane or no cane, I can do steps."

Noelle uneasily led the way up the three flights of stairs, then fumbled for her keys, wondering all the while why Alex was here.

She found out as soon as they were inside.

Alex pulled a newspaper article from his pocket. He snapped it open and began to read aloud.

"It's from today's paper. 'A major fossil discovery was announced yesterday by CMP paleontologist Dr. Noelle Forrest. Forrest, also know as Denver's Dinosaur Lady, has unearthed the jaw of an *Epanterias,* a rare dinosaur belonging to the *Allosaur* family.'"

Noelle gasped. Her eyes lifted to Alex's in confusion, but there was no reassuring expression in his as he continued to read.

Someone had called the papers? But who?

"'Dr. Forrest reports that more fossils may very well be in evidence on land owned by Matt Caldwell. A recreational therapist whose ranch caters to handicapped riders, Caldwell has been most generous in donating a previous find to CMP.'"

"Shall I read on?" Alex asked.

"Give me that." Noelle took it with trembling fingers and studied the article.

"You gave Matt your word! How could you go to the press?"

"I didn't!"

"Then how do you explain this?" Alex grabbed the paper from her and threw it to the floor. "How do you explain reporters calling us all day? Or the television cameras outside the front gates?"

"I—I can't."

"It was you!" Alex spat out. His knuckles turned white above his cane handle. "I told Matt you were no good! He—"

"That's not true! If anyone called the newspapers, it was you, Alex! You never wanted me at the ranch. I wouldn't put it past you to pull this stunt yourself and blame me for it."

Alex gripped his cane even tighter. "Don't try to pin this on me!"

Noelle took one look at his fevered eyes and gave up trying to defend herself. "This discussion is getting us nowhere, Alex. I want you to leave. Right now."

He shook his head. "Not until you admit you're guilty."

"I'm not. I'm innocent."

"Liar!" was Alex's angry cry. "You lied to my brother when you first came to the ranch, and you're lying now. Admit it! Admit it, or..." Alex moved across the room. He picked up a heavy hammer from her worktable and held it over her fossil.

Noelle froze. "Put it down, Alex."

"Why should I? You don't care about the ranch. You don't care about Matt's work. Why should I care about yours?"

"Is that why you came here, Alex? To make threats?"

Noelle slowly walked toward the table, but Alex raised the hammer even higher.

"Come on, Dinosaur Lady, come clean," Alex taunted.

Noelle shook her head. "I didn't call the newspapers," she said hoarsely. "Now put down the hammer, Alex! Violence never accomplishes anything!"

"I think you're wrong. I think a little violence will finally get us the truth."

Alex swung the hammer. Noelle cried out as his glancing blow chipped off a piece of fragile fossil, then she grabbed the hammer before he could swing again.

"Stop it!" Noelle screamed. "Let go right this instant!"

"No!" Despite his disabilities, Alex was stronger. "You came to our ranch and turned Matt's head with your pretty face. Now all he talks about is you. You and that brat of a boy have stolen him away from me!"

Alex tried to swing the hammer again, but Noelle yanked hard at the hammer and the blow missed.

"That's a lie!" Noelle gasped. "Matt will always be there for you. And even if he wasn't, you can take care of yourself! You're stronger than you know, Alex! Either way, you have nothing to fear from me!"

"Don't I, Dinosaur Lady? You want more fossils and you don't want to wait until spring. So you called the newspapers. Admit it!"

"I didn't lie to you! I didn't! You have to believe me!"

With all her strength, Noelle tried to wrench the hammer free. Alex finally dropped the hammer, sending Noelle flying to the floor. To her horror, she saw him lift the damaged fossil and hurry toward the window.

Noelle sprang to her feet. Grabbing Alex's waist, she pulled in the opposite direction with all her strength. Despite her best efforts, and even with his cane in one hand, he dragged her along in his wake.

"Last chance, Dinosaur *Liar*. Admit you called the newspapers or say goodbye to your precious fossil."

Noelle took one last frantic look at the fossil, and at the wild-eyed man who held it. There was no doubt in her mind. Alex was deadly serious about carrying out his threat.

"I kept my promise! I told no one about the dig site! Alex, please!" Noelle begged. "Don't do this!" She yanked at him again, and saw the bulky fossil almost fall from his hand.

But in a sudden, unexpected motion, Alex raised his cane and slashed at Noelle's face. She released his arm as her hands flew over her head in a totally instinctive gesture of protection. That was all the time Alex needed. With a mighty heave, he hurled the fossil at the window. The splintering sound of glass was followed by a sandstone blur.

Noelle screamed as glass and fossil fell three stories into the parking lot below.

And shattered into a million pieces.

CHAPTER TEN

THERE WAS SILENCE in the room. A dead, awful silence that seemed to last forever.

Noelle was the first to move. She raced for the door and ran down the three flights of steps to the parking lot, hoping against hope for a miracle.

Her hopes died as soon as she reached the asphalt. What had once been smooth fossilized surface and firm sandstone was now unrecognizable. A strangled cry escaped her throat, then died; so did her dreams. She knelt there, unmoving, in a numb agony that promised to get much, much worse.

Somewhere in the back of her mind she heard a car approach. Then there were voices—Alex's, Matt's. Still she didn't move. Matt approached her. She heard him at her side while she stared at the devastation. She saw him attempt to pick up fossil bits himself, then give up. She felt him carefully pick away the pieces of glass around her bleeding knees, even as her whole body trembled with shock.

And still she couldn't move. She was left with no fossil. No career. *Nothing.* "Oh, Noelle." Matt's eyes mirrored her pain, and something else she was too upset to see.... "I am—so sorry."

Noelle ignored him. She tried to gather what tiny shards were left into a pathetic pile, and pricked her fingertips with the glass.

"Noelle, don't. You'll cut yourself."

Matt reached for her hands, but Noelle snatched them away.

"Don't touch me." It was hard to speak, but even harder to accept his help. If only Matt had believed her about Alex, none of this would have happened. "I don't want you touching me," she repeated.

Matt's ragged, indrawn breath was followed by screeching brakes as yet another car pulled into the parking lot.

"We've got to get back on the sidewalk, Noelle. You're going to get hurt."

Noelle did look at him then. Didn't he know she was already hurt? That her own heart was lying in as many broken pieces as the fossil, along with all her hopes for the future?

"Please." He reached for her arm and gently pulled her to her feet. "Please come back inside."

Noelle's legs were shaking. She could make it only to the bottom of the stairs. There she collapsed, her eyes expressionless as they stared at the destruction before her.

There she remained. She didn't move when the apartment super showed up in response to a neighbor's concerned phone call. She didn't move when the handyman stepped around her and went upstairs with the replacement windowpane. She didn't even react when a white-faced Alex descended the stairs with a broom, dustpan and plastic trash bag.

She watched in silence as Alex struggled with cane and broom to gather up what was left. She averted her head as he awkwardly laid the bag at her feet. It wasn't until Matt tried to tend to her cuts with her own first-aid kit that Noelle rose to avoid him. She returned to her apartment.

The handyman was still working. Noelle went straight to her bedroom, shut the door in Matt's face and locked him out. She sat on the bed and buried her face in her hands, trying to block out his voice.

Finally, she could hear him no longer. She prayed desperately that he was gone. She heard the cheerful whistling of the handyman and wished he'd leave, too. She just wanted to be alone.

A few minutes later she heard the handyman call, "I'm all done, missy," and the front door slammed. Only then did she venture out of her room.

Noelle rose from the bed and unlocked the door. She stepped into the living room, then froze as she saw Matt. He was waiting for her on the couch, the first-aid kit in his hand. He rose as soon as he saw her.

Noelle couldn't bear to meet his gaze. Instead, her eyes took in the new window, the smell of fresh caulking still in the air. The carpet had been vacuumed, and her worktable was unusually clean—save for a shapeless plastic garbage bag. Noelle recoiled from the sight and sank limply onto her couch.

"Noelle . . ." His face was pale. "You're bleeding."

Noelle glanced down at her torn panty hose and cut knees, then at her bloodied fingers.

"Why don't you let me look at those?"

Under Matt's gentle ministrations her hands were swabbed and bandaged. Then, after she'd exchanged her skirt and hose for a pair of shorts, he took care of her knees. Yet the whole time she said nothing, even ignoring his low-voiced "I'm not hurting you too much, am I?" as he picked out the glass.

It wasn't until he asked, "Aren't you going to say anything?" that she responded.

There was only one thing she wanted to know. "Is Alex gone?"

"Yes. He's waiting downstairs." Noelle barely recognized Matt's voice.

"He threw—" *my fossil out the window,* she wanted to say. Only she couldn't get the words out.

"I know. Alex told me."

"Did he?" If she hadn't been so shocked, she would have been surprised.

"Yes. He told me about the fossil, the newspaper article . . . everything." There was a pause. Then, "He told me he tried to hit you."

Noelle shivered. "I don't want that man near me. Not ever again."

"Alex told me to tell you he's sorry. I know it won't bring back—" Matt broke off as looked over at her worktable.

"He needs help. Professional help. He scares me. Send him home, Matt. And go yourself."

"You want me to leave, too?"

"Yes."

There was a long pause. "I can't, Noelle, not until I know you're all right."

"All right?" Her voice rose a full octave. "After everything that's happened this evening, you expect me to be *all right?*"

There was a long silence. Then Matt finally asked, "Your knees . . . are they all okay?"

"They're fine."

"And your hands? You'll be able to work okay?"

"Work on what? That?" Noelle gestured toward the plastic bag on her worktable. She felt numb on the inside, numb on the outside, numb through and through.

"Noelle . . ."

"Still," Noelle interrupted, "I suppose I'll be able to type up my unemployment papers and update my résumé. Not that anyone's going to bother reading my résumé after today."

Noelle studied her hands in her lap. Only three of her fingers had escaped unscathed. Not that it mattered. She closed her eyes and wished herself a million miles away.

"Oh, Noelle, why didn't you just tell Alex you'd called the papers? That was all he wanted to hear. Instead you let him do this." Matt motioned toward the garbage bag. Noelle was surprised to see that his hand was actually shaking.

"So much for standing on principles. Look what it got me." Noelle could hardly believe she'd let Alex ruin the find of a lifetime. Yet the shattered evidence was right before her eyes.

"Why?" Matt asked in a strangled voice. "Dear Lord, Noelle, why?"

Noelle finally met his gaze. "Because in you, I thought I'd found something special. Something better than just that fossil. Something better than everything it represented. I'd hoped for so very much." Noelle's voice broke as that terrible numbness inside her started to fade. "I guess I was wrong."

Matt's eyes closed for just a moment, but long enough for her to realize that after all this time she'd *finally* made herself understood. Noelle prayed he'd now leave. But she was wrong. Matt refused to leave her in peace.

"Can you— Do you think you can salvage what pieces Alex saved?"

"*You* salvage them, Matt. I don't have the heart."

"What about us?" he asked hoarsely. "Do you think we can salvage what was between us?"

Noelle stared at him in outright disbelief. "Like what? Trust? Friendship? Anything at all? I think tonight proved there wasn't enough to start out with, let alone salvage."

A tremor seemed to pass through Matt's body. Noelle closed her eyes again, wishing him gone. But when she opened them, he was still there, still standing before her.

"Your brother's waiting, Matt. Go home."

But he didn't. "Do you really think you'll lose your job?"

"Which one?" she asked with a bittersweet smile. "The one at the museum? Or the one at the TV station?"

"If there's anything I can do to help...."

"You've done enough already." The accusation hung in the air. "Won't you please, please leave?" she begged.

Matt started toward her. As Noelle flinched, he stopped his forward momentum and clenched his fists at his side.

"And take that bag with you," she ordered. "I don't care what you do with it. Give it to Jason. Give it to the museum. Or throw it in the trash. I don't care. But I don't want to see it ever again."

Matt nodded. He reached for what was left of her hopes and dreams and slowly headed for the door.

"Matt."

Matt froze immediately in his tracks. "Yeah?"

"Did you really think I was the one who called the newspapers? Is that why you were coming over here? To get your pound of flesh, just like Alex?"

"Not exactly like Alex. But..." His voice trailed off. From the look in his eyes, she knew she had her answer. Still, she had to ask, "Didn't you trust me at all?"

"I did," he said. "Obviously not enough."

Noelle took in a deep, shaky breath and tried to ignore the pain in her chest.

"This is the last time I'm going to say this, Matt. To you—or to anyone. I don't know who called the newspapers. But I do know one thing. It wasn't me." She lifted her chin and looked him straight in the eye. "I didn't break my promise."

"I know that...now."

"Good. If anyone else asks you, tell them that. I may not have a career, but at least I'll still have my reputation. For whatever that's worth."

Matt's eyes fired briefly for just an instant. "It's worth a great deal, Noelle."

"Is it?" Noelle stared pointedly at the bag hanging limply from his side. "Is it really?"

Matt had no answer for that. He reached for the doorknob with his free hand.

"Good night, Matt."

Only it wasn't "good night." It was her "goodbye." And they both knew it.

"I'LL NEED YOUR museum keys and ID badge, Dr. Forrest. You're on thirty days' suspension without pay, effective immediately."

Noelle handed her supervisor the requested items. "And after my thirty days are up?"

"Do you want me to be honest, Dr. Forrest?"

"Please do."

"I'd start looking for another job."

Noelle took in the disapproving face of Dr. Peabody, her elderly colleague, who by now knew the whole story of the fossil's destruction. "Tell me something. Just what did you expect me to do to save that fossil? Jump out the window after it?"

"Whatever it took!" was his vicious answer. "I thought you were a team player, Dr. Forrest. I wish you *had* been the one to call the newspapers! At least then I could justify not suspending you!"

Noelle gasped. "That wouldn't have been ethical!"

"What does ethics have to do with anything when it comes to valuable finds such as *Epanterias!* There have been only three other partial specimens ever found! A *real* paleontologist would have used every trick in the book to save that specimen!"

"What tricks? Lying? Stealing? Breaking my word?"

"Whatever it took! Losing that fossil was unforgivable! I wouldn't have cared if you'd had to sleep with the ranch owner! Hell, if I was a woman, I would have!"

Noelle stared at her boss. A million replies crossed her mind. She discarded all of them. One look at her supervisor's face told her nothing would make any difference to a man like him.

"If that's what you honestly think, Dr. Peabody, I feel very sorry for you," she settled for saying. "Under the circumstances, I won't bother waiting a month to clear out my office. I'll be gone by the end of the day."

Her supervisor nodded. "I think that would be wise."

Noelle pivoted on the ball of her foot, and strode from the room. When she finally left her office with the last box of books, she turned around for one final look at the museum. She'd been beating her head against a wall for so long there—fighting to be included on digs, fighting for permission to work with real specimens instead of plaster casts, fighting to prove herself as a serious paleontologist.

And now, she was walking away from the fight. But instead of feeling sad and defeated, she felt a strange sense of relief. Surprised and just a little confused, Noelle headed back toward her car. She noticed that someone, probably security, had already scraped her CMP staff parking sticker off her car window. Despite this last indignity, Noelle smiled.

Maybe she'd never really belonged here in the first place.

Fortunately for Noelle's state of mind and bank balance, the studio workers and cast of *Fun with Fossils* were much more understanding. They were sympathetic, even outraged, at the unfavorable press.

Noelle was called into the station manager's office and personally assured that her studio job was in no danger.

"I'm sorry to hear about the museum firing you, Dinosaur Lady," Woody told her. "They had no right. And as for the newspaper coverage—well, I've seen better stuff in the tabloids!"

That was certainly true. Thanks to reporters who'd tracked down both her landlord and the gabby, whistling handyman, the whole sordid story about the destruction of the *Epanterias* jaw had been printed in the morning edition. Even CMP had contributed a comment. Reading between the lines, Noelle gathered that Matt had turned over the fragments to them. She was relieved that the Caldwell brothers had not been mentioned, although she herself had not been spared. According to the article and a museum spokesman, she was totally to blame for the fossil's destruction.

The quote read, "Dr. Forrest didn't go through proper channels, nor did she observe museum policies."

The consequence of being the official scapegoat was having her expulsion from the museum make front-page news.

Noelle couldn't believe it. Neither could the station manager. He acted even more upset about her situation than her family—and *they* were up in arms.

"Anyone who knows you won't believe that trash," he said. "Look, Noelle, I've called up a friend of mine at one of the network stations. Her name's Beverly Estrada."

He shoved a piece of memo paper her way. "Here's her number. Give her a call and tell her your version. She'll give you a chance to speak your piece."

Noelle took the paper, her throat tight with gratitude. "I don't know how to thank you, Woody."

He waved away her words. "If we were a network news station instead of an educational station, I'd get in front of the cameras myself and sing your praises. The nerve of the museum, firing you like that! Well, I'm sorry, Dinosaur Lady, but their loss is our gain. I've even talked to some people about going into syndication with *Fun with Fossils*. We've wanted more shows from you for a long time. Now's our chance to have them."

After one last pep talk, along with orders to stop by the legal department to check out her new contract, Noelle left his office. After all her heartache over yesterday's events, it was nice to know that *someone* appreciated her.

If only that someone could have been Matt....

But she hadn't heard a word from him. To her surprise, much of the public support had come from the children she met, and their parents. To her dismay, Jason Reilly hadn't been one of them. She'd tried to call him, but Mrs. Swanson had informed her that Jason didn't want to talk to her.

Noelle had even driven by the house, to be met with the same response.

"I think you should stay out of Jason's life," Mr. Swanson had bluntly told her on the front porch. He didn't even bother to invite Noelle in. "Jason was hysterical when he heard what happened to that fossil jaw. He doesn't want to see you, and personally, I think it's for the best."

The door had been firmly closed in her face. For a moment, Noelle had actually thought she might be sick.

That same day, thoughts of Jason, Matt and Alex made it almost impossible for her to maintain her composure on *Fun with Fossils*. But she forced herself to concentrate on the children. She even managed to finish taping a better-than-average episode, and was congratulating herself when she saw Alex Caldwell enter the studio audience.

Her satisfaction died the moment her eyes met his. Immediately she cut short her autograph session with a few polite words and a regretful smile to the children.

"I'm sorry, boys and girls, but that's all for today. Thank you for coming."

Noelle immediately headed for her dressing room, but despite his limp, Alex was right behind her, his hand on her arm.

"Please, Dr. Forrest, I need to talk to you."

"I think you've already said everything you needed to say, Alex. Now let go of my arm and get out of here before I call security." Noelle yanked away from him and continued down the busy hallway.

"I'm sorry about the fossil," Alex called out after her.

Noelle ignored him.

"Please, Dr. Forrest. I'm sorry you lost your job at the museum."

Noelle walked even faster.

"Matt wants to talk to you."

Noelle immediately stopped in her tracks and whirled around. "He can't deliver his own messages?"

"He can, but— Look, is there someplace we can talk privately?"

"If you think I'm crazy enough to be alone with you, you're sadly mistaken." Noelle gave Alex's cane a pointed look.

Alex flinched. He looked very, very young as his cane suddenly clattered to the floor. Younger than Jason, even. It was that fact, more than anything else, that changed her mind. Ignoring the curious stares of passers-by, Noelle bent over and retrieved Alex's cane.

She held it out for him. "This way," she said with a sigh.

Minutes later they were seated in the room that served as both office and dressing room. Alex looked miserable, but Noelle had no patience to spare. "I have a busy schedule, Alex. Say what you came to say so I can get back to work."

Alex swallowed, then began. "I want to apologize for trying to hit you yesterday. That was unforgivable. And I want to apologize for wrecking your fossil. It was a stupid thing for me to do."

"Stupid? That has to be the understatement of the year! You destroyed information that's millions of years old— priceless information that can never be retrieved or duplicated! How *could* you?"

There was a long pause. Finally Alex said, "I was scared. I think I've been that way ever since the plane crash. The only time I feel safe is when Matt's around. But ever since that fossil turned up, Matt hasn't *been* around."

"So you trashed the dig site to get rid of me?"

"Yes. And then, when I thought for sure you'd called the newspapers—I was determined to finish the job." He hung his head. "So I destroyed the fossil. I'm sorry, Dr. Forrest. I was wrong about you."

Noelle could have screamed at Alex's convoluted reasoning. "You've done more than just destroy a piece of history. You've ruined everything! The fossil, my career, any chance of a . . . friendship with Matt. And what about Jason? He won't talk to me, he won't even see me! I went to his house, and—"

Noelle wiped at the sudden tears on her cheeks. She couldn't go on. "I don't want to talk about this anymore. Go home, Alex."

But Alex stayed put. "Once I leave here, I'm checking into the hospital—a psychiatric hospital."

"Let me guess. This was another one of Matt's ideas."

"No, it was mine. I'll be staying there for a while until I can get my own place. That's my idea, too," he added. "Lord knows how I'll do on my own, but I think it's time I found out."

Noelle laid a comforting hand on his arm. The Caldwells had seen more than their share of misfortune, especially Alex.

Alex straightened up, and for a moment the look in his eyes reminded Noelle of Matt. "Look, I'm not here to cry on your shoulder. Or to ask for any favors for myself. I'm here for Matt."

"Matt?"

"Yes. The night we left your place, I thought Matt would be angry, Dr. Forrest. Furious, even. But he wasn't. Instead, my brother was..." Alex's eyes were full of pain. "I'll never forget the look on his face as we drove away. I know he blames himself."

"Did he send you here to say that?" she asked.

"No. But I do know he intends to see you." Noelle's heart gave a great leap, then fell again as Alex added, "It's about Jason."

"Jason?"

"Yes. He's canceled his riding lessons. Mrs. Swanson said Jason's not eating or sleeping well. He won't talk to anyone, not his foster parents or his social worker. Not even Matt. We're *both* worried about him. That's why I'm here— to ask you not to slam the door in Matt's face when he shows up."

"I wouldn't do that."

"Then you'll help Matt try and set things straight with Jason? Matt's going to bring him by, if the Swansons will let him. But if they won't, will you talk to Matt, anyway?"

"About Jason, yes."

"And about the fossil, too?"

Some of Noelle's anger returned. "Oh, Alex... What's the point? Thanks to you, there is no fossil."

"Maybe there's more of them. Maybe you just need to keep looking."

Noelle shook her head.

"You can't be serious! You'd just give up looking for more fossils?"

"Yes. In fact, the way I feel right now, if I never saw another one, it would be too soon."

"And Matt? Do you feel the same way about him?" Alex asked. "I know you care about him. You must, or you would have lied to save your fossil. Maybe you even... love him."

Noelle averted her head.

"Please, Dr. Forrest, say something!"

"I don't have to answer to you, Alex."

"You're right. But you sure as hell owe Matt and Jason some answers." For a moment Alex's old arrogance returned. "Tell me, Dinosaur Lady. Are you just going to walk away from everything?"

Could she? Noelle wondered. Walking away from her career would almost be easy compared to walking away from Matt and Jason. Because by doing that, she'd lose her heart. But what choice did she have without Matt's trust? And as for Jason—he only seemed to be fond of her TV persona, she thought sadly. The first time she'd messed up in real life, Jason had abandoned her.

"Noelle?" The arrogance was gone from Alex's voice now, replaced by desperation. "Don't give up. Maybe everything will work out."

She could only stare at Matt's brother and wonder, *Is there even a chance?*

CHAPTER ELEVEN

"THAT CONCLUDES OUR NOON report. Be sure to join us this evening for the news at five. For Denver's Round-the-Clock news station, this is Beverly Estrada, signing off."

The credits started scrolling up her television screen as Noelle reached for the remote control. She'd just shut off the set when the phone rang.

"I saw the news, Sis!" Molly raved. "You were great!"

"So you think it went well?"

"It sure did. All that TV experience sure paid off."

"I can't really take the credit," Noelle said. "It was Beverly's doing. I just answered her questions."

"Well, she knew her stuff. I loved the way she ripped into your supervisor for firing you. The museum came away with egg on its face. I still think you should have told Beverly about Dr. Peabody's disgusting suggestion on how to get more fossils."

"Molly, please! That's the last thing I want my *Fun with Fossils* fans to hear!"

"Well, at least call a lawyer," Molly urged. "This is your career we're talking about! I'm sure you have grounds for a suit."

"I don't know," Noelle said hesitantly. "The interview accomplished what I set out to do. It set the record straight. I wanted my fans to know that I acted ethically."

"You did that," Molly assured her. "I'll bet CMP gets hit with a wave of letters and phone calls by this time tomorrow. But you might still need a lawyer to help you get your job back."

"Maybe..." Noelle bit her lip. That much was true. But if she pursued a lawsuit, that would drag Matt and the ranch into the spotlight. Noelle knew a media circus was the last thing he'd want. To make matters worse, the thought of "sleeping with the ranch owner" was definitely appealing. Even though Noelle's motives were much more honorable than Dr. Peabody's, she didn't know if she could objectively discuss his crude conversation with any lawyer....

There was silence on the line. Then Molly said in a carefully bland voice, "It was awfully generous of you to mention on air that Matt needed more sponsors."

Noelle tried to ignore the way her breath caught at the mention of Matt's name. "Beverly was the generous one," she managed to say calmly. "I mean, we taped the interview. She could have edited that part out if she wanted."

"Well, I'm sure the publicity will do Matt's ranch some good." A delicate pause. Then she added, "Have you seen him lately?"

"Not since Alex destroyed the fossil."

"That was practically a week ago, Noelle! Has he at least phoned?"

"No." Noelle sighed. "I wouldn't know what to say to him if he did."

"Well, the least he could do is try to figure out who called the media, and go and break his or her neck. Then he should let me break *his*."

"I think you're carrying sisterly loyalty a little too far."

"Am I? Noelle, your fossil was ruined!"

You mean my life was ruined.

Noelle tried to ignore the pain in her heart. Her eyes moved to her desk, and the photo she'd taken of Matt and Jason at the dig site. She could do nothing but ache at their disappearance from her life, and reflect on what might have been. She'd lost more than her career aspirations. She'd lost the family she'd always dreamed of having. And she hadn't realized it until too late.

"Don't you have to check on your kids or something, Molly?"

"Not really, but I can take a hint. Look, call me if you need anything, okay?"

Noelle gently fingered the frame surrounding the photo. *What I really need is Matt. And Jason.* "I'll be fine."

"Are you sure? I can always drop the kids at Mom's and come over."

"Thanks, but no. I have to go now. Bye, Molly." Noelle firmly ignored her sister's last-minute fussing. She replaced the receiver and tried to work on her next script for an upcoming show. Two hours later, she was still on page one. Frustrated by her lack of concentration, she was thinking about shutting down her computer when she heard a knock.

"This had better be good," Noelle muttered as she made her way to the door. Since the newspaper article had appeared, more than one of her nosy neighbors had shown up to "chat."

She peered through the peephole and gasped. Quickly unlocking the dead bolt, she opened the door.

"Hello, Noelle."

"Matt. Alex said you'd be stopping by," she said awkwardly. Immediately she saw that there was a second person with him, someone her view through the peephole hadn't revealed. "Jason! Oh, Jason, I'm so happy to see you again. It's been too long."

Noelle received no response; the boy was uncharacteristically quiet.

"Can we come in?" Matt asked.

"Of course." Noelle held the door open wide, making room for Jason's crutches. "Please, have a seat."

Jason sat down next to Noelle on the couch. Matt continued to stand, her worktable starkly empty behind him. There was no denying the embarrassment of the moment.

"What can I do for you two?" Noelle asked after an uncomfortable pause.

"This won't take long," Matt replied. Was it her imagination, or did he feel as miserable as she did? There were circles under his eyes, and his face looked drawn and gaunt.

"First of all, I want to thank you for mentioning my ranch on the noon news. Our phones have been ringing off the hook with donations and sponsors. We'll be able to take on at least eight new students, maybe more."

Noelle smiled, her first real smile all week. "I'm glad, Matt. Beverly promised she'd run the segment again this evening."

"Secondly, I want to apologize for doubting you had the children's well-being at heart." Noelle started to murmur an appropriate response, but Matt cut her off. "Jason also has something he wants to tell you."

Noelle looked curiously at Jason. Suddenly his cheeks grew pale, and all animation was missing from his face. "Jason?"

Jason swallowed hard. He squirmed on the couch, studied his toes for a few minutes, then lifted his head and met Noelle's gaze. "I'm sorry, too, Dr. Forrest."

Dr. Forrest? Now she was really worried. Jason usually called her *Dinosaur Lady.* "Sorry about what, Jason?"

"I—I told the newspapers about the fossils on Matt's ranch."

Noelle's lips parted in amazement. *"You?"*

Jason nodded guiltily. "I looked up the number in the phone book."

Shocked, Noelle watched as Jason nervously adjusted the crutches he'd leaned against the couch.

"Tell her why, Jason," Matt ordered.

Jason hung his head. "Because I wanted to dig up more fossils, and Matt wouldn't let us. I thought if everyone knew about them, he'd change his mind."

"Oh, Jason...you *knew* we wanted to keep things quiet! If only you'd checked with me or Matt first. If you had—"

"We'd still have our *Epanterias* jaw, wouldn't we?"

"Maybe. It's hard to say." Noelle refused to make Jason feel worse.

But Jason wasn't fooled. "We would, too. I'm sorry, Dinosaur Lady."

Jason was manfully struggling to keep from crying, and Noelle slipped a consoling arm around his shoulder. Matt wasn't as lenient.

"You knew it was wrong to try to force me into letting you dig for fossils, yet you deliberately did it, anyway. I know that's not what your foster parents taught you."

Jason didn't take kindly to the lecture. Noelle felt him stiffen and mutter something under his breath.

"What was that, young man?" Matt demanded.

Jason lifted his head toward Matt, eyes mutinous. "I said it's your fault, too."

"Mine?"

Noelle didn't like what she saw on the boy's face. "Talk to me, Jason."

And with the primitive anger of a furious child, Jason did. "Matt thinks I'm a baby."

"I'm sure he doesn't."

"He does!" Jason cried. "I could make my horse take any trail I wanted! I could make him go around a dig site! I'm a good rider! But Matt doesn't think so."

"I never said that," Matt defended himself. "I'm just looking out for your safety."

"I can take care of myself! But you won't even let me off the beginner trails! I don't need a baby-sitter!"

Matt took a moment before carefully responding. "There's no shame in riding beginner trails. You'll advance to more difficult trails when I think you're ready."

"I *am* ready!" Jason's eyes were hard and accusing. "You treat me just like the Swansons did when I first came home from the hospital. Like I'm helpless!"

"Jason, I don't do that." For the first time, though, Noelle heard uncertainty in Matt's voice.

"You do! You do it to Alex, and you do it to me! And I hate that! So I called the newspapers to make you reopen the dig site."

"Sweetheart, newspapers rarely follow up on story leads from children," Noelle tried to assure him.

"But they did! I told them who I was, and I told them about your show. I even told them to call the studio for confirmation."

Noelle blinked. Jason's story had the ring of truth, and she'd learned long ago how resourceful he was.

"Jason, I still don't know exactly why you called the newspapers."

"Because then Matt would *have* to let us dig. And he'd *have* to let me ride a new trail! Only everything went wrong. It just made him mad. Then Alex got mad and broke the fossil. Then you got fired. And it's all my fault!" Jason lost the battle with tears this time. "I'm sorry, Dinosaur Lady. Please don't hate me."

Noelle blinked back tears of her own as Jason buried his face in her blouse. "I could never hate you, Jason. Please don't cry. I understand."

Continuing to murmur words of comfort, she held the boy tight and rocked him gently. No wonder Jason hadn't wanted to see her. He'd been afraid to face her! She looked up at Matt but he simply stood there, silent.

Finally she said, "Matt, come sit down." She patted a space next to her on the couch. "You and Jason need to talk."

Matt sat on the other side of Jason and lifted the boy into his own arms.

"Don't cry, Jason. You're right. This mess is my fault, too."

"I shouldn't have called the newspapers," Jason sobbed.

"And I shouldn't have made you feel frustrated." Matt's eyes were dark with emotion. "I didn't mean to hold you back."

Jason raised his eyes to Matt's. "I tried and tried to tell you, but you wouldn't listen."

"I should have. Others have tried to tell me the same thing." Matt sought Noelle's gaze over Jason's head. "I worried a lot when Alex was hurt. My parents had died, and Alex came so close to dying himself."

Jason swiped at his cheeks. "But Alex isn't a kid anymore, Matt. And I'm not a baby."

Matt paused. "You're right. I became very protective— overprotective—of Alex. I didn't mean to treat you that way."

"Then why did you?" Jason asked in a trembling voice. "You don't do that to the other riders. Did Alex make you hate me?"

Matt shook his head, and in a blinding flash Noelle realized the truth.

"No, Jason. Matt doesn't hate you." Her eyes met his. "In fact, I think it's just the opposite. He cares for you so much he doesn't want anything to happen to you. He looks out for you because he loves you, Jason."

Jason turned toward Matt. "Really?"

"Yes."

"You held me back because you were worried about me?"

"Yes, Jason. Noelle's right—the way I would love my own son. That's how I think of you, as a special son. I love you. I know I'm not supposed to get emotionally involved with my patients, but I couldn't help it with you. And then I started to worry...." When Matt spoke again, his voice was firm. "Perhaps if I'd realized that sooner, none of this would have happened." He shook his head. "Don't feel bad, Jason. Your intentions were honorable, even if your methods weren't."

Noelle could see that Jason didn't quite understand the last sentence, but he did understand what Matt meant when he drew him close and hugged him hard. The tears stopped, although the worried expression on his face still remained.

"What about your job, Dinosaur Lady? Will your landlord evict you? Will you have to go on welfare?"

"Heavens no, Jason," Noelle assured him, marveling at the concern in the boy's voice. "I still have my job at the studio." She ruffled Jason's hair as he relaxed a little in Matt's arms. "Don't you worry about me. I'll be able to pay my rent, and then some."

"But every paleontologist needs a museum affiliation. You said so on your show."

He was right about that, Noelle thought with a pang. But before she could answer, Matt spoke.

"She might get her job back, after all, Jason."

"Matt, don't raise his hopes," Noelle warned. "I probably won't."

"You will if Molly and I have anything to say about it."

"Molly?" Noelle said at the same time as Jason's, "Who's Molly?"

"Molly is Dr. Forrest's sister. I called her a few days ago to see what I could do to help. At my insistence, Molly told me of a certain... unpleasant conversation you had with your supervisor, Noelle."

Noelle closed her eyes in embarrassment and wished she could slink under the couch.

"I won't repeat it here," Matt said in tones that were diamond-hard, "but suffice to say it provided my lawyer with plenty of ammunition."

Noelle opened her eyes. "*Your* lawyer?"

"Yes. He and I paid a visit to the museum on your behalf. I wasn't going to mention it until he got back to me, but I'm sure we can correct matters."

"Really?" Jason brightened perceptibly. "Is the man who fired the Dinosaur Lady in trouble?"

"Oh, yes." Matt's dangerous smile held no warmth. "I can safely say he is. We'll get our Dinosaur Lady back where she belongs."

Noelle stared at Matt. Matt had hired a lawyer for her? She didn't know what to make of the news, but Jason sighed with happiness.

"Feel better now?" Matt asked the boy.

Jason nodded.

"Everything will be fine. I promise." Matt's words included her, too, but Noelle wasn't so sure. She reached for a tissue from the end table and handed it to Jason. It wasn't until Matt's digital watch beeped the hour that anyone spoke again.

"You should get downstairs, Jason. I asked Mrs. Swanson to meet me here," Matt explained at Noelle's look of inquiry. "She's probably wondering what's taking so long."

Jason nodded. Noelle started to reach for Jason's crutches, which had fallen to the floor, then froze at Matt's warning look.

"It's okay, Matt," Jason said with a smile. "I don't mind if *she* helps. My foster mother says women can't help fussing sometimes."

"Mrs. Swanson is a wise woman," Matt remarked as Noelle passed Jason his crutches.

"Goodbye, Jason." Noelle watched him adjust the crutches. "I'm glad you stopped by."

"And thanks for being honest," Matt added. "You've given me a lot to think about. We'll talk when I see you tomorrow. Same time, same horse."

The boy's eyes opened wide. "You're not mad at me? You're still gonna let me ride?"

"You bet. But this time we'll try an advanced trail." He held out his hand. "Do we have a deal?"

Jason solemnly shook Matt's hand. "Deal." Then he struggled to his feet from his position on the couch. Once he was standing, he addressed Noelle.

"I'm sorry I messed things up, Dinosaur Lady. I should have talked to Matt or you before I called that reporter. Mr. Swanson says I act first and think later. He says I always have to learn things the hard way."

He glanced down at his braces with a profound sadness she'd rarely seen in a child. Then that sorrow was gone, replaced by firm determination as Jason looked her straight in the eye. "I'm not going to be like that anymore. I know it won't fix your *Epanterias* fossil. I know it won't get your job back, either. But I'm going to try, anyway—just for you."

Noelle was deeply moved. She had to clear her throat before she could respond. "You do that, sweetheart. But don't do it for me."

Jason tilted his head in confusion.

"Do it for yourself, Jason. Do it for *yourself*."

The boy studied her for a long moment. Then his eyes glimmered with understanding.

"I promise—Noelle."

Suddenly, Noelle knew that she would never be the "Dinosaur Lady" to him again. But even as regret swept through her, it was replaced by a fierce feeling of pride. Because—just for a moment—Noelle Forrest caught a glimpse of the fine young man Jason would some day become.

And she wouldn't trade that honor for all the dinosaur fossils in the world....

"Come on, sweetheart. I'll walk you to the door," she said softly. She stood up, as did Matt.

"Bye, Matt."

"Bye, Jason."

Noelle let Jason open her door for himself, but couldn't resist saying, "Be careful on the stairs."

Jason magnanimously allowed that warning to pass without comment. Instead, he flashed her a grin and descended the stairs, with Noelle following after. It wasn't until he was back in his foster mother's car and driving away that Noelle closed the door against the cool evening air.

Matt was still waiting in her apartment.

"That's some kid," he commented.

"The best."

"You're very good with him."

"You were, too, tonight," Noelle said. "I think he'll be fine."

"What about us, Noelle?"

Noelle couldn't find the words to answer. She honestly didn't know what to say. What *did* two people say when a shaky relationship foundered?

"I see," Matt said after an uncomfortable moment.

"Matt, I need some time to think."

"There's no need to explain," he said wearily. "I've been stupid, but I'm not that stupid."

Noelle bit her lip, wishing she could erase the past, yet knowing she couldn't.

"Before I go, Noelle, I just wanted to let you know that you have my permission to dig on my ranch. Any place, any time. I've decided to reroute the creek-bed trail to allow you full access to both the banks and the bed."

"But—what about the patients? And your horses? You said..."

"I know what I said," he interrupted. "However, my horses are well schooled. With the proper handling, they'll adjust to a new trail. This will be a healthy challenge for my more advanced riders." He paused, then added, "The change will do them good. I don't want to make things too easy for them. Like I've been doing for Jason. And Alex. It's time to correct that.''

Noelle felt her heart swell with pride at Matt's admission. "You're doing the right thing, Matt."

Matt nodded. "Like I said, you can dig anytime. Just call the office.''

"Thanks. Maybe I'll take you up on that next spring.''

"Next spring?"

Noelle nodded. Somehow she couldn't work up the old excitement. Too much had happened. Matt hadn't trusted her until she'd stood by and let Alex destroy her work. She'd lost Matt and her fossil, not to mention her museum job, then suffered through Jason's pain when he'd blamed himself. And yes, she even felt sorry for Alex. She was physically exhausted and emotionally drained.

"Why wait? It's early enough in September to dig before winter sets in.''

"I'm just not up to it." That much was true. "The way I feel right now, if I never saw another fossil, I wouldn't lose any sleep over it."

"But finding fossils is what you do!"

"Is it? I wonder..." Noelle mentally compared the single fossil she'd found with all the children she'd met over the last few years. "Maybe it's what I *did,*" she muttered. "Matt, I want you to call off your lawyer. I want him—and you—to stay away from CMP."

"You can't let them fire you without a fight!" Matt was incredulous.

"I won't have anyone, not your ranch, not your patients—and especially Jason—subjected to another media blitz. The price is too high."

"Noelle, this time you *have* to think of yourself! Don't quit now!"

"I'm not quitting at all."

"But..."

"This is my personal business, not yours. I'll handle it my own way."

Matt seemed to capitulate. "As you wish."

Noelle opened the door again. "I do appreciate the thought, though."

His lips twisted in a bittersweet smile. "Gratitude isn't exactly what I wanted for the two of us. And as far as I'm concerned, this isn't over...not by a long shot."

Noelle knew he was waiting for a response, but she didn't trust herself to reply. Finally Matt stepped out of her apartment.

And left without a backward glance.

CHAPTER TWELVE

"Restricted Entrance—CMP Staff Only."

Noelle looked away from the familiar sign and reached for the spare museum key in her purse. A curt message on her answering machine had requested its return immediately. She'd retrieved the key from her desk at home and planned to drop it off on the way to another taping session of *Fun with Fossils*.

With a self-deprecatory twist of her lips, Noelle inserted the key and turned it. Technically she was still employed. She hadn't received her termination papers in the mail yet.

Noelle passed a few members of the museum staff on her way to her supervisor's office. Much to her surprise, those same co-workers hailed her with welcoming smiles and friendly greetings. By the time she reached her destination, she was totally confused. Not one person had chastised her for losing the *Epanterias* fossil.

Her confusion grew when she entered her supervisor's office and found *his* supervisor waiting there.

"Good morning, Dr. Forrest."

Noelle nodded. "Good morning, sir. I'm here to return my duplicate key to Dr. Peabody. Have you seen him?"

"About Dr. Peabody... Do you have time to talk?"

"I'm sorry, but I don't," Noelle replied in a chilly voice. She gave her wristwatch a pointed look. "I'm on my way to the studio. Perhaps I can leave this with you?"

"I must insist on a few minutes of your time, Dr. Forrest. You see, I've been in contact with your lawyer."

"I don't have..." Noelle suddenly broke off. Obviously Matt hadn't done what she'd asked.

"I've been made fully aware of your supervisor's remarks and his policies," Dr. Maddox went on, his lined face serious. "Let me assure you they are not this museum's policies. Dr. Peabody's comment to you was more than just sexist. It was unconscionable. So much so, in fact, that he's no longer with us."

"No longer—?"

"Dr. Peabody resigned rather than face the scandal that our pressing charges against him would have caused. We'll be filing a retraction in the newspaper, too. The museum not only extends its apology, we want you to fill the vacancy his departure has left."

Noelle was flabbergasted. "Replace him? As supervisor?"

"Yes, both here at the museum and out at our dig sites. We hope you'll accept."

"Dig sites? You want me out at the dig sites? I don't believe it. You aren't being forced into this by Matt's—I mean, by my attorney?" Her response prompted a rush of words from Dr. Maddox.

"This is a bona fide job offer, Dr. Forrest, not some legal ploy to appease you."

"You really want me back?"

"Your ethics are above reproach," Dr. Maddox said earnestly. "With people like you working for us, our museum's reputation and credibility will remain intact. It's more than time for you to give up your TV work and become an active member of CMP. I only regret not realizing your potential sooner. We'd be honored to retain your services."

Noelle's fingers closed tightly around the key in her hand. Finally, after all these years, the brass ring was almost within her grasp!

All she had to do was reach right out and grab it....

Noelle took a deep breath. "I appreciate your offer, Dr. Maddox. But I must refuse."

"Refuse!" His face paled. "You still intend to proceed with your lawsuit?"

"No, sir. I don't." Noelle watched relief appear in the older man's eyes, then give way to confusion.

"But...Dr. Forrest, I don't understand! I thought you'd be pleased!"

"I am pleased, more than you'll ever realize."

"Then why not accept our offer? You're certainly qualified for the job."

"I know that. But good as I am with fossils, I've realized that I'm even better at—"

"Working in front of the cameras," he finished impatiently. "Yes, yes, we've all seen *Fun with Fossils*. You've certainly made the most of your skills as a paleontologist there. But now it's time to use them for the museum."

"I'm sorry, sir. You have it all wrong."

Dr. Maddox blinked. "You're *not* a skilled paleontologist?"

"Oh, I'm a competent paleontologist, all right. But I've learned that's not where my true talent lies."

"What are you saying, Dr. Forrest?"

"I'm saying I'm a teacher. What's more, I'm a damn good teacher. I can't—won't—give it up."

She felt a moment of sadness at leaving her old dream behind. But then she thought of Jason's face and of all the other young faces whose lives she'd touched, and the regret passed. It was time—more than time—to move on.

"It would be wrong to deny who and what I am, Dr. Maddox. I'm going to continue doing *Fun with Fossils*."

"You'd rather work for some low-paying educational station than be a fully tenured museum curator and supervisor?" His voice rose in disbelief.

"Yes." Noelle gently placed her office key on the desk.

Dr. Maddox stared at it. Obviously he wasn't ready to accept her decision. "Don't be foolish, young woman! There's no way any viewer-supported station can match the salary or prestige of the position we're offering you!"

Noelle gave her boss an indulgent smile. "It's not the money."

"But we want you at the dig sites!"

"There's so much more to paleontology than just dig sites, Dr. Maddox. I'm sorry, but my answer remains the same."

Dr. Maddox groaned and shoved the key toward her. "At least tell me you intend to keep your affiliation with us."

"I'd be honored." Noelle picked up the key, slipped it into her purse and held out her hand. Dr. Maddox shook it with great reluctance.

"Well, if you change your mind..."

"I won't." Noelle rose to her feet. "Goodbye, sir."

Dr. Maddox morosely watched her head for the door. "Goodbye, Dr. Forrest."

"Not Dr. Forrest." She lifted her chin and sent him a brilliant smile. "I'm the Dinosaur Lady."

"CHANGE OF PLANS, Dinosaur Lady!" the assistant director yelled through the open door of her dressing room. "I hope you're ready."

"For what?"

"We're going live again today."

"Live? Why *this* time?"

"Our new sponsor likes it that way."

"Is this the same guy who wants to syndicate me?"

"That's the one. He says going live makes for a more spontaneous show. He's got the bucks that feed our budget, and this isn't the networks, so..." The assistant director shrugged.

Noelle sighed. "Great."

"It gets worse. We're going on location."

"On *location?* Where?"

"To that horse place."

Noelle felt her heart skip a beat. "Please tell me it's not the Caldwell ranch!"

"That's the one."

"I didn't authorize any location shoot! Why wasn't this cleared through me?"

"Woody set everything up for a location shoot through Matt Caldwell. We're all ready."

"Matt was here? Today?"

"Yep. Said to make sure to tell you he'd be in the audience. Along with the new sponsor. There's a van and camera crew waiting out front."

Despite her worry about doing a live show, Noelle felt a flutter of excitement at the prospect of seeing Matt.

The ride out to Matt's place was nerve-racking. For once Noelle couldn't join in the good-natured banter of the camera crew. She couldn't even concentrate on reviewing her script. Perhaps she should have taken the museum's job offer, after all. Because if she had to go live with Matt watching, her boss, her sponsor and all her viewers would see Denver's Dinosaur Lady make a fool of herself—live and on the air. She'd lose her TV job for sure!

"Hey, Dr. Forrest, isn't this where we turn for the ranch?" one of the crew asked, startling her.

Were they here already?

They were. "Take the next right," she confirmed.

"Here we go," the driver announced a few minutes later. He parked the van in the lot just outside the office and shut off the engine. "We'll wait here for you."

Someone slid open the door nearest her. Noelle suddenly realized she was expected to go inside and finalize whatever arrangements had been made.

"Something wrong, Dinosaur Lady?" one of the cameramen asked, seeing her hesitation.

That had to be the understatement of the year....

She shook her head, then stepped onto the pavement. With any luck, Matt would be off with his patients somewhere. "I, uh, I'll be right back," she said, fighting the butterflies in her stomach.

Noelle took a deep breath and walked through the automatic doors. Much to her surprise, the office was empty.

Except for Matt—who was waiting for her at the reception desk. He rose to his feet before the doors had even closed behind her.

"Hello, Noelle."

"Matt." She nodded in response, hating the way her pulse raced at the sight of him. "I'm supposed to talk to you about today's shooting location?"

"That's right."

"Well, just tell me where to send the crew, and I'll let you get back to work." She glanced around the empty office, then faced him again. "Although it looks awfully slow today."

"Is that all you can find to say to me?" Matt asked.

"Well, I could always complain about your meddling," she said irritably. "Like your going behind my back with your lawyer at the museum or making arrangements with Woody for today's location shoot."

"We're doing your show here to help boost your popularity."

"Matt, don't be ridiculous! That's going to take more than a live shoot at a worthless dig location."

"I intend to try. Since it's my fault you lost your job, it's my responsibility to get it back for you."

"I got it back, along with a raise in salary and position, thanks to that lawyer of yours. The same lawyer I told you I didn't want."

"I'm glad. You should never have been fired in the first place."

"Don't start celebrating yet. I turned down the offer."

Fierce triumph was replaced by confusion on Matt's face. "You turned it down?" he echoed incredulously.

"Yes. I discovered I didn't want it, after all." Noelle watched his expression turn to shock.

"After everything that's happened? Why?"

"I started thinking about Jason and the influence I've had on him. I started thinking about all the other children who watch my show. A new job at the museum couldn't begin to offer the same satisfaction as the work I'm doing now. So I decided to refuse it. I did keep my affiliation."

"At least you have *that* much sense. You can't tell me you don't care about finding fossils anymore."

"I have lots of sense, and of course I care! But I've decided to concentrate on what I do best. If being on television means I have to leave the fossil finding to someone else, well, I can live with that."

Matt actually had the nerve to smile at her. "Well, Doctor, as long as you know what you're doing."

"I'm managing my professional life just fine," she retorted.

"And your personal life? Is everything 'just fine' there, too? Haven't you missed Jason? Haven't you missed me? Because we've certainly missed you."

"I—" Her voice trailed off under Matt's assessing scrutiny.

"Noelle ..." Matt reached for her just as the van's horn beeped long and loud. Noelle whirled around to peer through the glass doors, and the moment was lost.

"The crew is waiting for me, Matt. I assume we're headed back to the old dig site?

He neither confirmed nor denied her question. "I'll ride down in the van and show you where to park."

"That won't be necessary."

"I'm not welcome?" he said with raised eyebrows. "On my own land?"

"Quit putting words in my mouth! It isn't that! But this location shoot was sprung on me at the last moment. My script was written for the studio. I'm going to sound stupid doing it out here." Noelle ran shaking fingers through her hair. "So if you don't mind, I'd prefer you weren't around to watch."

Matt's eyes glittered. "You have nothing to worry about, love. I swear it."

Noelle blinked at the determined expression on his face. *Love?* What in the world was going on? "But Matt..."

Her words were drowned out by another blare from the van's horn. Matt came around from behind the desk and reached for her hand.

"Come on, Dinosaur Lady. It's getting close to airtime."

Noelle let Matt lead her outside. He continued to hold her hand during the ride. She didn't know what to make of that, so she looked out the window as the van bounced along the dirt trail leading toward the creek bank. Her eyes opened wide as she saw all the buses and parked vehicles.

"Good crowd today, right, Dinosaur Lady?" one cameraman said.

"And then some," another replied. "I heard the new sponsor's coming to watch today, too. See him sitting next to Woody? He and Woody are talking about revamping the show and renaming it *Around the World with Fossils.*"

"But our station doesn't have the money for that!" Noelle protested.

"It will if Woody can get you picked up by the networks! So make us all look good, Dr. Forrest." The first cameraman winked. "If you get a raise, we might have chance at one, too."

Noelle bit her lip, then felt Matt's reassuring squeeze.

"Pull over right here, please," Matt told the driver. "This is as close as we're going to get."

Her palms began to sweat as she smoothed her skirt, then climbed out of the van. She lost sight of Matt as people surrounded her and the familiar routine began. A mike was clipped to her lapel, her hair and makeup were touched up, and the director approached to start barking out directions. "Where are my cue cards?" Noelle asked in a panicky voice.

"You won't be needing them," the producer guaranteed her. "Just follow Jason's lead."

"Jason Reilly?"

"Yes. He's your guest co-host today. He and Matt Caldwell have everything planned out. Trust me, you'll like it."

Where *was* Matt? Why was everyone smiling? What was going on?

"Ten minutes, Dinosaur Lady. Everyone, places!"

Noelle looked frantically around at the crowd of school children sitting on the rows and rows of folded chairs. She swallowed hard and put on a brave face. As she walked toward the creek bed, she realized this wasn't the old dig site. But before she could question anyone, the children spotted her.

Murmurs became gasps, then excited words once she was recognized. Noelle looked out at the crowd, then spotted

Jason Reilly in the section roped off for the show. He was also waving and calling to her.

"This way, Dr. Forrest!" he called, balancing on his crutches. "We have to get down inside the creek bed."

An already anxious Noelle heard the words with trepidation. She wasn't dressed to go climbing. Neither her high heels nor Jason's crutches were made for steep banks. The only thing worse than falling flat on her face would be watching Jason get hurt.

"Hurry up, Dr. Forrest! It's almost time for the show to start!"

Noelle increased her pace. As she did, she started noticing other faces in the crowd.

"Molly?" Sure enough, it was her sister, accompanied by her husband and children. Noelle's parents were there, too. All gave her broad smiles and large waves.

Noelle picked her way through the creek bed. Then she saw Alex. He was sitting away from everyone in a folding chair, but he waved when he saw her. So did the Swansons, and their two daughters.

Noelle weakly waved back and continued to study the crowd, seeing familiar faces from both the museum and the television studio. Most of Matt's younger students from his special riding classes had come, too. So had the members of Jason's boys' club. They all seemed to be waiting for something. Then Noelle reached the edge of the creek bed and saw why.

Her hands flew to her cheeks. *It couldn't be ...*

The trail that had formerly covered the bottom of the creek bed was gone. In its place, right below the old creek loop where she'd found her jaw, was a carefully sectioned dig site, complete with grid after grid of partially exposed fossils.

"Did we surprise you, Dr. Forrest?" Jason asked excitedly. Despite his braces, he was practically hopping from one foot to another. "Did we?"

Noelle was more than surprised. She was speechless. She went on staring at the huge bed that had been dug, the numerous specimens exposed to the bright sunlight.

"I was in charge of the dig site," Jason proudly announced. "I told everyone what to do."

"You did this, Jason?" Her eyes locked on the massive finds lying below her feet in the new dig site.

"I helped, but mostly I supervised. Matt and Alex did most of the work. Matt found the fossils, and Alex organized the workers."

"Matt? And Alex?"

Jason nodded vigorously. "Yep. Once Matt found this place, Alex called me to come organize the dig. And I asked all my friends at the boys' club and here at the ranch to help, too."

Noelle still couldn't believe her ears. "Matt was digging for fossils?" she repeated.

"Uh-huh. He was out here every day. Even in the dark. He let Alex run the ranch. If you don't believe me, ask him."

Releasing one crutch, Jason happily gestured toward the opposite side of the creek bank. Noelle's breath caught at the sight of the man standing there alone.

Matt.

"*You* did all this, Matt?"

"Not alone. Everyone pitched in."

"For *me*?"

"They all love you, you know." Matt's deep voice carried across the deep creek bottom separating them. "I know I do."

"You—love me?" Noelle took a step closer to him, then stopped as she reached the edge of the creek bank.

"Yes. Oh, yes. But I was too proud, too cautious, to admit it. I thought you didn't understand how much my work meant to me. I thought we had nothing in common. But I was wrong." He gestured toward all the rows of children. "We have hundreds of things in common."

Noelle's arm went around Jason's shoulders. "We do, don't we?" she said, her voice husky with emotion.

"I'm very glad you think so." A slow smile crossed Matt's lips. "Under the circumstances, I think it's time we re-opened our negotiations," he said. "The fossils and I are a package deal. You can't have one without the other. And you have to promise to love me more than you do them."

"You drive a hard bargain, Mr. Ranch Owner," she finally managed to say.

"You haven't answered my question."

The whole audience strained to hear her. Most missed the actual words, but it didn't matter. Noelle's expression said it all.

"I do love you, Matt. But I have to warn you, I have a package deal of my own." She placed her arm around Jason. "We're a team. Jason goes where I go."

"I can accept that. In fact, it sounds as if a merger is in order." Matt's smile now spread to his eyes. "But only on one condition. When it comes to any deal, we're talking lifetime contracts here. You, me and Jason. No loopholes. No options. No cancellations. Do we have a deal?"

Noelle turned toward the trembling child at her side. "What do you say, Jason? Does that sound like something you could live with?"

His fierce hug was her answer.

Then Matt was scrambling down the side of the creek bed, while Noelle and Jason did the same, high heels, crutches and all, until she and Jason were in Matt's arms, kissing, being kissed, and crying and laughing, all at the same time.

Noelle's heel snapped off and came to rest outside a grid rope. Jason dropped a crutch near an exposed fossil surface. She didn't care. The only thing that mattered was Matt and Jason, and the way they held her tight.

"I love you, Dinosaur Lady," Matt whispered, pressing a kiss against her temple. "You, too, son. You're the best things that have ever happened to me."

"Don't give me any halos," Noelle immediately replied. She backed away just enough so she could see his beloved face. "I have my faults just like everyone else."

"You won't let me put you up on a pedestal?"

"A pedestal?" Noelle laughed with joy, the sound rippling through the air. "Please don't. I get enough of that as the Dinosaur Lady. For Jason, I just want to be Mom. And for you, Matt, just plain old Noelle Forrest. Think you can live with that?''

The cameras rolled and the young audience broke into whistles and catcalls as Matt gently set Jason aside, pulled Noelle closer and kissed her thoroughly.

"I most certainly can," he murmured.

"FINALLY!" MATT SIGHED. "I thought they'd never leave."

"And I thought Jason would never go to sleep," his Dinosaur Lady added.

"Our boy was on adrenaline overload. Hell, the whole ranch was. What a zoo!" But there was no anger in Matt's voice, just relief that it was over.

It was after midnight, and the two of them were nestled on his couch for some well-deserved rest.

"It's been a pretty eventful day for him. Let's see." Noelle counted on her fingers. "Jason was on live TV, was offered a permanent position as my assistant, found out he was being adopted, learned we were getting married, and heard me agree to riding lessons from him for a wedding present . . . all in one day."

She dropped her hand and snuggled against his chest. "You can't expect any child—or adult, either—to fall asleep after something like that!"

"No, I suppose not. But still, I was getting very tired of waiting to do this." Matt kissed her long and leisurely, followed by several light kisses for good measure. "Fossils and TV cameras are all well and good, but right now I prefer peace and quiet, with Jason asleep, and you all to myself."

Noelle smiled and managed to say, "Me, too," before her lips were occupied with something other than words. It was quite some time before there was any more conversation.

"I only wish we'd done this a lot sooner," Matt finally murmured. "It would have saved us both a lot of grief."

"I don't know." Noelle's expression was pensive. "We've both been so lucky, considering everything was such a mess. I was confused about my two jobs, about what I wanted to do. And the situation between you and Alex was so mixed up."

Matt sighed. "I'm not proud of myself when it comes to that."

"Matt, you did what you thought was right. Now you've stepped aside to let Alex take care of himself. He says he's moving into his own place on the ranch, and he's staying with his counseling. It's a good start."

"I think so. And speaking of Alex, I didn't get a chance to tell you. We've had a long talk, he and I. I'm going to turn running the ranch over to him."

"Is Alex up to that?" Noelle asked uneasily.

"Alex and his therapist think so. He did just fine while Jason and I were out at the dig site this past week."

Noelle nodded. Although Alex had profusely apologized to her, Noelle wasn't as comfortable around him as she wished she could be. Still, the prognosis for a complete emotional recovery was promising. For both Alex's and Matt's sake, Noelle hoped that day wasn't too far off.

"Alex was always a better rancher than me," Matt continued. "I'd rather devote all my time to my patients and lobby group, anyway. And Jason. And most of all, you." He kissed her tenderly. "Alex wants it that way, and so do I."

"I've learned a lot about myself, too," Noelle said softly. "I was so busy chasing after one dream that I almost walked away from the one staring me in the face. A dream that has everything to do with you, Matt, and with Jason and with how much I love you both. I've also learned that I'm a good teacher. It's the thing I do best. And it took you and Jason to make me realize that."

Matt sat up straight. "That's why you quit the museum?" he said with sudden understanding.

"Yes. And now Woody and the new sponsor are determined to repackage *Fun with Fossils* as *Around the World with Fossils*. They're positive they can get the networks to pick us up. In the meantime, I've been offered more shows and airtime. *And* they'll let Jason be my permanent co-host."

"An international Dinosaur Lady. Of course you're going to accept," Matt said, his face filled with pride.

"Of course. Colorado isn't the only place to find fossils, even if we do have the Morrison Formation. There's Canada, and China, and France, and..." Noelle sighed blissfully. "Think how many children I'll be able to reach."

"I don't know if I like having to compete against all those fans." His forehead wrinkled in a mock frown. "We may have to add a rider to our deal."

"And what would that be?"

"I get top billing in your entourage. Will you let me add that to our merger?"

She gave him a slow, Mona Lisa smile. "I think I can agree to that."

"Well then, Dinosaur Lady." Matt tenderly pulled her back into his embrace. "Let's seal our new agreement now."

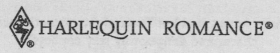

HARLEQUIN ROMANCE®

brings you

Stories that celebrate love, families and children!

Watch for our next Kids & Kisses title in October.

**Sullivan's Law
by Amanda Clark
Harlequin Romance #3333**

A warm, engaging Romance about people you'll love and a place that evokes rural America at its best. By the author of A Neighborly Affair and Early Harvest.

Jenny Carver is a single parent; she works too hard and worries too much. Her son, Chris, is a typical twelve-year-old—not quite a kid anymore but nowhere near adulthood. He's confused and bored and resentful—and Jenny isn't sure how to handle him. What she decides to do is take him to Tucker's Pond in Maine for the summer—a summer that changes both their lives. Especially when they meet a man named Ben Sullivan....

Available wherever Harlequin books are sold.

Where do you find hot Texas nights, smooth Texas charm and dangerously sexy cowboys?

Crystal Creek reverberates with the exciting rhythm of Texas. Each story features the rugged individuals who live and love in the Lone Star state.

"...Crystal Creek wonderfully evokes the hot days and steamy nights of a small Texas community...impossible to put down until the last page is turned."
—*Romantic Times*

Praise for Bethany Campbell's *The Thunder Rolls*

"Bethany Campbell takes the reader into the minds of her characters so surely...one of the best Crystal Creek books so far. It will be hard to top...."

—*Rendezvous*

"This is the *best* of the Crystal Creek series to date."
—*Affaire de Coeur*

Don't miss the next book in this exciting series. Look for
GENTLE ON MY MIND by BETHANY CAMPBELL

Available in October wherever Harlequin books are sold.

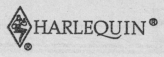

THE VENGEFUL GROOM
Sara Wood

Legend has it that those married in Eternity's
chapel are destined for a lifetime of happiness.
But happiness isn't what Giovanni wants from
marriage—it's revenge!

Ten years ago, Tina's testimony sent Gio to
prison—for a crime he didn't commit. *Now* he's
back in Eternity and looking for a bride. *Now*
Tina is about to learn just how ruthless and
disturbingly sensual Gio's brand of vengeance
can be.

THE VENGEFUL GROOM, available in
October from Harlequin Presents, is the fifth
book in Harlequin's new cross-line series,
WEDDINGS, INC. Be sure to look for
the sixth book, **EDGE OF ETERNITY,** by
Jasmine Cresswell (Harlequin Intrigue #298),
coming in November.

MIRA™

The brightest star in women's fiction!

This October, reach for the stars and watch all your dreams come true with **MIRA BOOKS**.

HEATHER GRAHAM POZZESSERE
Slow Burn in October
An enthralling tale of murder and passion set against the dark and glittering world of Miami.

SANDRA BROWN
The Devil's Own in October
She made a deal with the devil...but she didn't bargain on losing her heart.

BARBARA BRETTON
Tomorrow & Always in November
Unlikely lovers from very different worlds...they had to cross time to find one another.

PENNY JORDAN
For Better For Worse in December
Three couples, three dreams—can they rekindle the love and passion that first brought them together?

The sky has no limit with **MIRA BOOKS**

Fifty red-blooded, white-hot, true-blue hunks
from every State in the Union!

Look for MEN MADE IN AMERICA! Written by some of
our most popular authors, these stories feature fifty of
the strongest, sexiest men, each from a different state in
the union!

Two titles available every month at your favorite
retail outlet.

In September, look for:

WINTER LADY by Janet Joyce (Minnesota)
AFTER THE STORM by Rebecca Flanders (Mississippi)

In October, look for:

CHOICES by Annette Broadrick (Missouri)
PART OF THE BARGAIN by Linda Lael Miller (Montana)

You won't be able to resist MEN MADE IN AMERICA!

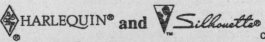